I0664338

AN ALTON OAKS' MYSTERY

In the
Dead
of
Winter

by
Megan Rivers

For information, email Cozy Cat Press, cozycatpress@gmail.com or visit our website at: www.cozycatpress.com

COZY CAT
PRESS

ISBN: 978-1-952579-13-4
Printed in the United States of America

10 9 8 7 6 5 4 3 2 1

To my favorite photographer (and fairy godmother)
Sue Conwell who lives in color but, like winter,
captures the beauty of life in reflections of black & white.

PROLOGUE

RIGHT AFTER A LATE AND HEAVY autumn rain, the streets of Sheridan looked slick as the raindrops coated the sidewalk and newly paved asphalt road of First Street. Maddie Prince's curly red hair peeked out from beneath the hood of her raincoat as her black galoshes splashed in the fresh puddles. She was rushing to the tri-city bus stop. Rain drops still fluttered to the ground as the breeze rustled them loose from the trees.

The days had grown drastically shorter as well as colder. Maddie's breath rushed past her lips in a billowing cloud as a shiver ran down her spine. The intermittent yet strong gusts of wind that rushed between the quiet buildings brought tears to her eyes as she adjusted the strap of her backpack. The AP books weighed down her faded red Jansport.

Moments like these—the quiet atmosphere of freshly fallen rain and the lack of extremely watchful or judging eyes, would normally make Maddie's shoulders relax. The tension of her senior year of high school would run away from her momentarily. She couldn't, however, shake an odd feeling that had put her on edge since she left

Sheridan's Public Library; she got shivers when the clock above the bank next door chimed seven times.

Her galoshes splashed through the streets, disturbing the muffled town. They echoed off the buildings—until she heard another noise that wasn't coming from her feet. The tri-city bus stop was at the end of the block, brightly lit under a nine-foot tall street lamp. She longed to be under its safe illumination, but her feet were frozen in place as her ears strayed to hear the noise again.

Her Irish green eyes scanned the raindrop-spattered cars parked along the curb and the dim storefronts. Business owners were turning their signs to *closed* and shutting off lights—if they hadn't done so hours ago. An orange tabby dashed across the street from beneath a black pickup truck and Maddie let out her breath, convincing herself that all she'd heard was the stray cat chasing its dinner.

The local tavern, O'Brien's, was dark, but Maddie knew it would be open for several more hours. She stood in the shadows, letting her heartbeat slow as she watched someone exit the bar. An old man with thinning gray hair stepped out of the heavy wood doors. She watched as he seemed to sniff the air and pulled out a small metal container of chewing tobacco. He shoved a wad of the same vile stuff her father always used, and fished out a small ring of keys from the pocket of his well-worn, and stained Carhartt overalls.

Maddie didn't urge her feet to move yet as she stood beneath the awning of the pharmacy. She watched the man wobble down the street, swerving into a fire hydrant once and grabbing a hold of a nearby lamppost as he approached his dented, rust-covered car with a missing bumper. It was only after the sound of his loud car disappeared into the night that Maddie dared to move again.

The tri-city bus would arrive at 7:30—the last bus of the night. She had time before it arrived and was grateful for a few extra moments to work on her Calculus practice test before morning. The thought of studying minimums, maximums, and derivatives distracted her from the noise she'd heard before. As her mind was consumed with the Extreme Value Theorem, she neglected to recognize the hairs of her arm standing on end. Her ears didn't register the footsteps trying to silently move on the sleek, rain-covered pavement.

Maddie was only a few yards from the bus stop, her mind thinking about a problem on the practice test that had stumped her at study group. Her mind had drifted elsewhere as a cold, clammy hand reached out from the shadows. All at once, math facts escaped her mind as a hand covered her mouth and two strong arms pulled her backwards, deep into the depths between the barber shop and the pharmacy. The poor seventeen-year-old girl didn't even have time to scream.

Automatically, Maddie reached for the cold, grape-scented hands that covered her mouth. Her eyes wildly searched the darkness around her, not yet adjusted to it. Her heart beat wildly and as she felt the heavy lump of her backpack, put space between her and her attacker. She used it as a weapon, pushing the weight of it backwards, arching her back to maximize the space between them. Managing to peel the hand from her face, she turned wildly to face her assailant, her curly red hair turned frizzy from the struggle and the rain sprinkling down from young maple trees along the street.

"Maddie, relax!" a familiar voice pleaded. She saw his palms in the air as his brown eyes filled with concern and sorrow for what he'd done.

"Jesus, Jason!" Maddie exclaimed, her body shaking with adrenaline as she adjusted the book bag on her shoulders. "You scared the living daylights out of me!" she exclaimed, clearly irritated.

"That was kinda the point," Jason said and ran his hand through the damp tendrils of hair on his head. "I didn't know you'd freak out like that," he shared, opening his arms for an apologetic hug.

Maddie's lips grew thin—a sure sign she hadn't gotten over the prank—as she looked up and down his dark lean figure, ignoring his gesture. She rolled her eyes as she pulled frizzy locks behind her ears that had escaped from her French braid. "Sorry," she apologized for no other reason than it was a habit. "I just have a lot on my mind." She turned and let herself be drawn into the safety of the light at the bus stop.

Jason followed Maddie and sat beside her on the metal bench. He leaned back and draped his arm behind her as she hunched forward, the book bag still clinging to her shoulders. "Is it the history project or the AP Calc exam?" he asked. He knew her better than anyone; the boy next door who'd chased her, despite her father's bellowing and red-faced, ham-fisted warnings.

During their childhood, they'd shared a treehouse deep in the maple trees behind their houses. It was built by someone who'd long since moved away. Jason would stash his savings from cutting lawns in a metal box, and bury it beneath the roots at the base of the tree so his alcoholic mother wouldn't find it. Maddie would use the treehouse as a safe house when she needed to escape her overbearing father. It was the little house they shared together as children. Once in a while they'd use it still; Maddie could always tell Jason had been there because he'd leave behind an empty package of chewing gum (usually the Bubble Gum Tape—grape flavor, in the purple container).

"Come on, Maddie," Jason said, playfully elbowing her in the shoulder. "I know you've spent the past week in the library before school, after school, and during every lunch period. You're stressed out and always hidden behind notecards or a book. This is the first time I've seen your entire face in days."

Maddie bit her lip as Jason spoke. She knew being seen with him was a risk, especially if her father found out, but he was such a good friend—her best friend—and dare she say it?—her secret boyfriend. "Both, if you must know," she answered and then sighed. "And neither," she added.

"I *need* to be valedictorian, Jason," Maddie admitted with tears rimming her eyes. Her expression struggled between a mask of normalcy and a breakdown. They weren't quite halfway through the school year, but Maddie had to keep tabs on her standings in order to give that speech during graduation in the spring. "My dad will kill me if I don't get it. Wendy and I are neck-and-neck. We're always so close. I can't have a repeat of what happened in eighth grade," Maddie admitted, thinking back to when Wendy had transferred to Sheridan Junior High in the beginning of eighth grade and snatched valedictorian from Maddie. She could still remember how angry her father was. She couldn't relive that.

"I have to ace the calc exam to pull ahead," Maddie said and rested her head in her hands, looking down at the spots of black gum on the sidewalk between her galoshes. "I'm just so tired of being so scared of doing the wrong thing."

Jason put a supportive hand on Maddie's shoulder. She let tears fall down her cheek before falling into his embrace on the bench. "You'll ace it, Mads," he reassured her. His long pale fingers rubbed her shoulder as she pulled away, wiping away any trace of raw emotion from her face.

"And don't worry about your dad," he added. "You'll escape him soon enough; I'll be sure of it. College is just around the corner. And..." he paused for a moment before continuing, "I knew you were always the one who'd make it out of here."

How many times had they had this conversation before? How many times had Maddie tried to calm Jason down as he stomped through the trees around their treehouse, seething, fuming at his mother? How many times had he come upon the treehouse and heard those heart-breaking wails and weeping from her best friend? Was it ever going to end?

Maddie could see her reflection in Jason's glassy brown eyes. Warmth rushed through her. She loved him. It was different than the way she loved her grandmother or loved the smell of rain. "Jason, I..."

Her sentence was cut off by a terror that slashed through her like a machete. A gray, boxy, 1985 Pontiac— the type of car that was dependable and cheap in its day— had turned onto First Street; its headlights sweeping past them like a searchlight. Any normal person would've nodded in approval at how well cared for the car had been, despite the rust spots around the tires—the result of driving too many years on salted roads during Midwest winters. Maddie and Jason knew better. They shot up from the bench knowing what was coming wouldn't be pleasant.

Already Maddie's heart beat faster and sweat pooled on her temples, despite the chilly breeze that rippled through the street with the arrival of the car. It was the same engine, the same muffler, the same sound that had sent terror through her when it had pulled into the gravel driveway of her house each day. The same headlights that swept past her bedroom window as she prayed that he wouldn't slowly open her bedroom door and wake her up after seeing that his wife was in a deep sleep. Panic and anxiety always traveled with that Pontiac.

"Dad," Maddie stated. She tried not to stutter or let her voice falter in any way as the car came to a stop at the curb in front of them.

A shudder shook her shoulders. Maddie felt like she was shrinking as she stepped away from Jason. She naively hoped her lifelong friend wouldn't be noticed as the driver's side door creaked open.

As an ex-high school football star, Maddie's father still sported a large healthy frame, though he had a bald spot on the top of his head, which he tried to hide with a comb-over. His large black boots stomped over the puddles along the curb. The buckles clinked with each step. His lack of speech was menacing to Maddie as she stood in his shadow.

"I stayed late for a study group," she stammered. "I have a big calc exam tomorrow."

Her father's eyes took in the way her hair started to come lose from her hairstyle and curled with the nervous sweat that ran down her temples. His brushy eyebrows narrowed when he took in the teenage silhouette of Jason. An eight-year old memory of her father chasing Jason out of their backyard as they were eating popsicles dashed in front of her eyes.

"Get in the car!" he bellowed. His voice was the kind that dove deep and pierced quickly, like the horror in Hitchcock's movie *Birds*. Even Jason could see how shaken Maddie was as her father approached, and it fueled a fire inside of him. He noticed how her hands, as they peeked out from the sleeves of her rain coat, began trembling, and how she slouched, trying to make herself smaller; to disappear.

When neither teenager moved, the man grabbed his daughter's pale wrist. "Get in the car, Madeline," he demanded and pulled her along.

Maddie glanced at Jason over her shoulder with an apologetic look before she stumbled across the curb. Her father tugged her once more, off the curb and into the street. Maddie didn't have the courage to glance back at Jason, once she was shoved into the backseat and under the careful glare of her father's eye in the rearview mirror. She clutched the strap of her backpack and recited the Table of Elements in her head to distract her from what was to come.

The red glare of the Pontiac's brake lights illuminated the fury in Jason's face as he helplessly watched the scene. He wanted to help Maddie because even though they were only seventeen years old, he knew with every feeling he ever felt that she was the love of his life. And she deserved so much better

Chapter One

THE SNOW FELL SOFTLY, LIKE NOTES to a lullaby. The sun hadn't risen yet, but the sky was bright against the stifling clouds.

Winter used to be my favorite season; building a family of snowmen in the front yard, sledding down Blackhill Avenue, sipping on the secret Alton family hot chocolate recipe in Mom's hand-painted snowman-themed mugs, and (of course) Christmas. It would be the one time a year I'd come to Alton Oaks and visit my family. It had been two years since my last snowy visit and I should've been excited, but I wasn't. I couldn't get out from under this heavy cloud of depression. My thoughts and moments were consumed with the absence of Jackson.

Yes, I'd left him almost eight months ago and that was difficult. I felt like I was just getting a handle on my emotions and finding a direction. Then everything changed. It had been nearly two months since his horrific passing, but I couldn't work past it. It was like I'd come to a speed bump that I just couldn't get over, no matter how hard I tried. Jackson was my first love, my husband, and he was gone. Despite the horrible things he'd done and how he'd made me feel, I still mourned him.

The sky outside my bedroom window began to dull. Hues of red and orange began to crawl through the clouds. It would be a perfect day to go ice skating in Sheridan or hide in a corner of the Alton Oaks library—perhaps near the crackling fireplace—and get lost in a world that wasn't my own. Yet I didn't even have the energy to turn away from my bedroom window. With the blankets pulled up to my ears, I let a few tears fall on my pillowcase.

December was supposed to be fun—a month of excitement and festivities. I just couldn't bring myself to participate this year. I could still remember my first winter in Costa Rica, after I'd joined the Peace Corps. It was my first December without snow. Ever. And I missed it. December always brought snow, and with snow came festivities and family time. None of that was on the agenda in Latin America. It was also a day in December when I first met my late husband.

I was leaving my placement at a local school for the day. The commute to my host family was long and, despite the sun shining and San José registering a balmy seventy-seven degrees, I was miserable; culture shock had finally set in.

Then there was Jackson. His pale face and strawberry blonde hair stuck out right away in the small entrance of the building. Of course, his hair was longer then, held back in a ponytail, and highlighted by the sun, but his smile was the same. "Hey," he said and caught up to me in a few steps.

I was taken aback by the attention; I even glanced behind me, thinking his greeting was meant for someone else.

"You're Charlotte, right?" he asked. I didn't correct him. After I left Alton Oaks, I didn't correct anybody. I wasn't Charli anymore; I was Charlotte.

"Yeah," I said hesitantly.

"You just started, right?" he asked, following me out the door.

It was nice hearing English words outside of my head. I nodded, squinting at the sunlight on the pot-holed streets. "Yeah. I was just transferred from a farm in Pozos. I've been in Costa Rica for a few months," I explained over the noisy town.

"Do you like it?" he asked.

Again, I nodded, catching a glimpse of his smile from the corner of my eye that made me blush. "I do," I admitted, despite the bout of homesickness. "It's a lot of fun."

"Where're you from?" he asked as we passed a stray dog lying in the corner of a doorway.

"Illinois," I responded, sneaking another glance at his wintry blue eyes. They reminded me of the ice covered pond at the Miller's farm in Alton Oaks.

"Chicago?" he asked, enthusiastic.

I shook my head. "No. Western Illinois. Not far from the Iowa border."

"Are you like a farm girl?" he asked with humor. Why does everyone always assume that? It was getting exhausting.

"No. Where are you from? California?" I made the assumption based on his looks and the fact that most of the Americans I met here were either from California or New York.

Humor illuminated his chuckle. "No, El Paso."

Before I could follow up with a comment on sombreros, he changed the subject. "Are you taking the night classes?" he asked as we rounded a corner. The smell of coffee and the stomach-rumbling sight of boiled red pejibayes slathered in mayonnaise diverted my attention for a moment.

"Night classes?" I asked, passing by the food vendor with regret.

"They're offered through the Peace Corps to get your ESL and TEFL certification. You should look into it; you're a natural," he said with a smile that sent excited shivers across my shoulder blades. I'm sure my cheeks would have blushed if they didn't seem to be permanently pink with sun exposure since my arrival.

"Thanks," I said, wondering if he even caught a glimpse of my class or if he was just being kind. A shy smile crossed my lips and I tried to hide it by looking down the road before crossing. "What is it you do here?"

"I'm coordinating futból leagues for the inner city kids," he explained as we arrived at the bus stop. "The kids at your school have their first match on Saturday. If you're interested, I can save you a spot on the sidelines."

I hadn't been asked out on a date since David Martin had asked me to prom my senior year of high school, and I stumbled over a response as my bus barreled down the street.

"Meet me here," Jackson said, cutting me off, pointing to the corner where I waited every day for the bus. An attractive air of confidence accompanied his words. "At eight on Saturday, if you're interested."

Flattered by his attention, I nodded at his request with a smile as the bus pulled up. After boarding, I watched Jackson from the window: the clean cut line of his jaw, the positive energy he radiated, the way his wintry blue eyes never seemed to squint at the sun, and how his broad shoulders let the rest of his t-shirt hang loosely around his frame. As the bus lurched forward, leaving Jackson behind, I knew I'd see him again; I knew he'd be a permanent fixture in my life and I smiled at that.

Sometimes you just *know* and so much of the universe that was an enigma suddenly made perfect sense.

There was movement on my twin-size bed and, for a moment, I woke thinking I was in my bed in Albuquerque—that this was one of those moments when my heart fluttered, excited that Jackson had actually returned home in the middle of the night. How many times did I toss and turn throughout those nights with the false hope in my past life—my pre-widowed life?

Opening my eyes, I first saw the weak morning sun reflecting off the snow balancing on the tree limbs outside my window. Realizing that this was my post-life in Alton Oaks, I saw that the movement came from my best friend Sadie before she even said, "Good morning, sleepyhead!" Cold air still radiated from her jeans from being outside in the blowing wind.

Sadie's morning visits didn't happen every day, but I was glad when they did... otherwise I wouldn't have gotten out of bed. "Look what I found in today's paper," she said, reaching her arm across my shoulder and dangling this mornings edition of *The Oak Leaf Press* a few inches from my face. "It's another Charli Parker photograph!" she said with pride.

I sat up slowly, against my white wicker headboard, clutching the newspaper, shoulder-to-shoulder with Sadie on the small bed. The headline of our local newspaper read: *Ice Fishing Early on the Whett River.* My photograph was below it: a black and white candid of two old men outside a hut, holding their bounty. Sure, it wasn't hard-hitting journalism, but this was news in Alton Oaks. It was a small confidence boost when I saw one of my photographs in *The Oak Leaf Press*, though the audience was a fraction of the fifteen hundred people that made up our town.

I'd been freelancing for the newspaper since the Miller's Harvest Table event at the end of November. Seeing my name at the bottom of the picture on the front page made me feel like I belonged to Alton Oaks again. Ever since I'd returned to my hometown eight months ago, so much tragedy had occurred because of me that I began to feel alienated, though I'm sure most of it was in my head.

The old mattress rocked gently as Sadie rolled off the bed. I leafed through the four-page morning issue hoping to see another one of my photographs as Sadie walked over to my closet and opened the creaking door. My spirits lifted as I saw another photograph of mine that covered the holiday decorations on Main Street and the Meet Santa event that the Oakie Doughkie Bakery & Gift Shop holds every year.

"I'm taking you out for coffee," Sadie said as a midnight-blue sweater hit me square in the face. She tossed a pair of pants at me and added, "The Buzz is doing a cookie decorating contest today with the Oakie Doughkie Bakery. First prize is a free coffee and doughnut every Sunday for a year!" Sadie moved to my dresser and threw a t-shirt at me. When I groaned at the idea of going out in the cold weather, she turned and said, "And if free coffee and sugar doesn't appeal to you, bring your camera. You can always get some shots for the newspaper."

My eyes glanced from the Nikon on my desk, to the sky outside. It was a great day for photographs with freshly fallen snow and a blue sky. The clouds that blanketed the dawn had dissolved. Even if *The Oak Leaf Press* didn't take any of the pictures, it would make me feel better. I was tired of the exhaustion and unwelcoming emotions that lingered since Jackson's passing. I knew it wasn't going away any time soon and it was healthy to go through the stages of grief, but I so badly wanted to get on with my life. Hiding behind the lens of my camera helped me see the world with different eyes and it was almost healing.

"Okay," I said to Sadie, giving in. I threw the blankets off my body and automatically felt the chill that invaded the old house.

"Ten minutes," Sadie instructed with enthusiasm and threw the hard-water stained towel that hung off my desk chair at me. "I'll meet you in the truck."

Chapter Two

TEN MINUTES MIGHT HAVE TURNED into twenty minutes as I hesitated getting out of the hot shower. I didn't think Sadie noticed as she was rocking out to the local country music station, blasting on the speakers of the truck that sat on the Alton House front lawn. I watched her auburn hair fly around as her head bobbed; she sang along to a song whose muffled notes I could hear from the porch stairs.

The snow came up to the riding rail of her truck. The tires sat nearly buried in the snow. Since neither of my parents had a car—they preferred walking or biking to their jobs in town—we had no reason to shovel the long driveway at the east end of Oak Street. My brother's Jeep and Sadie's pick-up were the only cars that trekked this far and they had no problems traversing the snow and ice.

As my snow boots left the salted stairs of the Alton House, I saw the ten yards of deep foot prints that Sadie had left behind and I followed them, only making my own path in the soft snow when I reached the front fender.

Opening the door, a welcoming blast of warm air erased the chill that crept onto my cheeks. I pulled myself into the cabin and Sadie turned down the music. "What do you want to listen to?" she asked, her cheeks pink and her eyes bright, as I slammed the passenger side door shut.

Sadie knew I was tired of being asked how I was doing, if I was all right, and all the other questions I didn't know how to answer. So, she took to asking what kind of music I wanted to listen to—once even when there was no radio around—to gauge how I was doing. Oddly, it worked for me. I knew how to answer that question; it wasn't hard to reflect my mood through a song. "Country is fine," I said, glad I didn't want to hear anymore Papa Roach.

"I heard that Sheridan's Snow Jam is supposed to have ZV perform," Sadie informed, turning to me and wiggling her eyebrows. Sharing gossip was a favorite pastime of the citizens of this town, and Sadie enjoyed asking questions. I think that's why she and my mother got along so well.

"Geez," I said, shifting through memories. "I haven't been to the Snow Jam since sophomore year of high school." The next town over, Sheridan, throws their annual winter festival every February and it was a huge event in western Illinois. They earned most of their tourism income for the year during the two weeks of the music festival, despite the chilly temperatures and accumulating snow fall.

"I figured as much. And I cannot believe they have someone as *huge* as ZV coming to the bash: Zachary Verne himself!" she giddily exclaimed as we made it onto Oak Street without getting stuck in the snow. Sadie hit the gas and was not the least bit concerned about ice on the unsalted road.

ZV is a very famous country singer who grew up close to Sandalwood—a town about forty-five minutes from Alton Oaks. He's a huge celebrity in this part of Illinois. As Sadie talked about the rumor and other news she heard about the festival through the grapevine, I took off my gloves and pulled out my camera as the dashboard vents were pouring out heated air in full force.

I did my normal routine of cleaning the lens, checking the settings, and taking a test picture of the snow-covered cemetery as we passed. I began scrolling through the photographs on my memory card. They were all pictures I'd taken in the past five months. I had to surrender my last memory card to Jake, the town deputy, this summer when I was a murder suspect, and I had yet to get it back. It contained photographs from my life outside Alton Oaks: my life with Jackson. I was suddenly grateful that I didn't have it; I didn't want to churn up the memories of loneliness and heartbreak.

"You'll still be in town, right?" Sadie asked, snapping me out of my thoughts.

"Sorry, what?" I asked as Sadie pulled into the packed parking lot behind Froz T's and The Buzz Coffeeshop.

"To go to the festival," Sadie said as she carefully pulled her monstrous vehicle into a parking spot beside the brick wall of the fish, game, and boating supply store: Hook, Line N' Sinker. With such a tight squeeze, I'd undoubtedly have to climb over the console and exit out of the driver's side door. "You'll still be in town in February, right? I can get us tickets to go to Snow Jam this year," she informed, shifting the gear into park and looked at me questioningly.

"Oh," I said, trying to think about the feasibility of my presence as I packed away my camera. When I first returned to Alton Oaks, I wasn't sure if I'd planned on staying, but now it seemed as though I had nowhere else to go... I just didn't want to admit that. I wasn't sure if I wanted staying to be my long term plan. "Sure," I said, avoiding eye contact. "Let's go to the festival."

Navigating around snow banks and braving the chilly morning air, we made our way onto Main Street where there was already a line out the door of The Buzz. Sadie and I huddled together in the line of parents and red-cheeked children. As the line crept to the door, the warm sugar-and-coffee-scented air caught on the breeze near the threshold.

The Buzz started this cookie-decorating tradition after the Robinsons opened the Oakie Doughkie bakery in 1999. As a ten year old, I tagged along to the first one when my mother took my younger sister, Bailey. Back then it was a folding table set up near the counter with a sign made of construction paper and permanent markers that designated one cookie per twenty-five cents. Now, there were time slots and each cookie was a dollar. Despite the steep price, the town handed out money because all proceeds went towards the children's wing at St. Colette's Hospital on the west side of town. Sadie was a nurse there and as we waited in line, she told me about the history of the event—all the things I missed, spending so many years outside of Alton Oaks.

"I got you a ticket," she said and handed me a red card stock rectangle with clipart and a large ADMIT ONE: 9:15 A.M—9:45 A.M. emblazoned on the front in bold letters. "This is how the hospital can afford the Snow Social for the kids. It pays for the toys, cookies, hot chocolate, and decorations. The kids love it. Do you want to volunteer with me on Christmas Eve? I usually meet up with your family at church afterwards."

Before I could give a noncommittal nod, Mrs. Willis— my old Sunday school teacher who looked like Mrs. Claus in a festive holiday sweater—held out a hand with a jingly, Christmas-themed bracelet on her wrist. Happily, Sadie handed over her ticket and I did the same. We spilled into

The Buzz which was packed with loud families. I automatically took out my camera to hide behind the lens.

Sadie and I made a beeline for the counter of specialty coffees and I couldn't have shoveled out cash from my pocket any faster for two large cups of the dark Viennese Strudel. With my camera hanging around my neck, I stood in a quieter corner of the shop, and wrapped my hands around the warm cardboard cup, officially beginning my day. Taking a deep breath of the sweet-scented caffeine, I watched as the rest of the world moved in fast-forward around me.

"I love it, Sadie," I said as she showed me her fifth decorated cookie. I took a picture of it next to the one she'd dressed in festive lederhosen. After snapping the shudder a few times, I noticed that in the twenty minutes we'd been there, I'd taken over one hundred photographs.

"I don't know," Sadie said, tilting her head as she studied the very dapper snowman she'd dressed in blue and white frosting—the facade of a tuxedo. "I think the sugar sprinkled on top makes it too gaudy. I'm going to try another one." Sadie glanced at the large coffee-cup shaped clock on the wall and said, "We still have time."

Sadie and I have been best friends since Kindergarten and I knew I couldn't stop her from thinking her cookie was imperfect, no matter what I said. I watched her hand another dollar over for a sugar cookie and let her spend the last ten minutes wedged between nine-year-olds with fists spattered in icing and sprinkles.

Christmas music played over the speakers placed all around the coffee shop. The Reading Tree bookshop was attached to The Buzz and the regular morning caffeine patrons had to help themselves from a makeshift coffee bar nestled between the shelf of biographies and Illinois history. I wandered over to the small cordoned off partition, thinking that a photograph of the change of morning services might be useful to *The Oak Leaf Press*.

After taking a picture, a voice called out from beside the table of confections and pastries. "Charli Parker!"

Pulling the camera away from my face, I saw a woman in a long red apron waving in my direction. She stood behind the table adorned with the green and pink labels of the local bakery. Her white curly hair was held back with a black clip and her cheeks still seemed pink from the temperature outside. I tried to place a name with her face as I walked over to the table full of wide-eyed children pulling on their mothers' coats for an extra treat.

My eyes swept over the thickly frosted cupcakes topped with baby candy canes, the white chocolate peppermint bark, the slices of sugar cookie cheesecake, nestled among the carefully detailed and colorfully decorated cookies. My stomach quaked in response, wanting a bit of a sugar rush.

Confusion was probably apparent on my face because after I approached, she responded, "Oh you probably don't remember me. I'm Sophia Robinson." She took a moment to smile at a child marveling at the display of mini cupcakes covered in edible glitter. "We met way back when you were in high school doing volunteer work for the food shelter."

No hint of recollection crossed my features as I searched through trunks of memories. "My husband and I own Oakie Doughkie Bakery," she added.

Immediately, I remembered going into the bakery with my Uncle Dan after church in his old green Volkswagen Beetle on Sundays, before he moved to Milwaukee. We would buy an Angel Food Cake for the table, and he'd buy us chocolate-filled wafer cookies for the ride back home. Even as a teenager, I enjoyed this sugary act of rebellion against my mother's "No food between church and dinner!" rule. Mrs. Robinson would always greet us with a warm smile and give us a free sample of the freshest cookies.

"Oh yes!" I said, kind of remembering her during one of my many volunteer shifts for my honor society credits. "How are you?" I asked, moving against the wall as a large family of children congregated at the table.

"Oh, just great," Mrs. Robinson shared. She held her left thumb in her right palm—a tick or trait that was familiar. Sometimes she'd rub her thumb in her palm, or choke it with her fingers. I guessed it depended on her stress level. She held it gingerly as she continued, "My daughter took over the gift shop next to the bakery a few years ago, so I get to see her and my granddaughter every day now. It's been wonderful."

While I tried to think of what establishment was formerly beside the bakery—was it a photography studio? That ill-fated, pet-themed boutique?—her eyes traveled down to the camera in my hands. "I see you've been keeping yourself busy since you've been back in town. I've been noticing your name more and more in the newspaper," she commented and placed her hands in the candy-cane striped pockets of her apron.

I blushed, hoping she wasn't insinuating my name being associated with the deaths that had occurred in our normally sleepy town... especially the latest one of my husband. To my relief, Sophia added, "Just this morning one of your photographs made the front page, didn't it?"

I nodded. "Yes. It's just a hobby, but it helps me pass the time, and I enjoy it."

Mrs. Robinson took off her latex serving gloves as if the idea that was illuminating her face needed more room to glow. "The week before Christmas each year, Greg—my husband—dresses up as Santa and we invite families to come into my daughter's gift shop and take pictures. Our regular photographer was the girlfriend of a mechanic at my son-in-law's shop in Terryville, but she married and moved to Des Moines last month. It was quite unexpected for everyone," she said with a hint of disdain, as if there was more to the story that she wasn't sharing. She quickly rebounded and asked, "Would you be interested in filling in? It would only be for a week. Noon to eight on weekdays, seven to four on the weekend. We split the cost sixty/forty on pictures purchased."

I had no plans, no temporary jobs lined up, no family or community commitments, so I don't know why it took me so long to respond. "Just for a week?" I asked, and she nodded, hopeful. "Yeah, I guess that would be okay."

"Great," she responded, her thin ruby red lips pulled into a smile and she handed me a snowman-themed cake pop. "Thank you! Here, on the house," she said, handing it to me. A teary-eyed, three-year-old watched the transaction in the arms of his mother.

Sadie appeared at my shoulder just in time to share my treat. "You might want to come by an hour early on Friday to set up your camera and printing supplies. We'll have the set all ready for you." Sadie raised her eyebrows at me in question. "Oh," I said, taken aback at the added responsibilities, but I guessed that a professional photographer would be responsible. "Okay. Yes," I agreed. "It would be helpful to check the lighting and troubleshoot any technical problems," I added, hoping it hid my surprise.

Sadie grabbed my elbow just as the cow bell rang, signaling that our ticketed session at The Buzz was over.

"Nice to see you again, Mrs. Robinson," Sadie said,

waving as we retreated.

"You too, pumpkin," Mrs. Robinson replied with a smile as last minute customers waved their money at her, desperate for a purchase before they were ushered out of the store.

"Are you working for the bakery?" Sadie asked as we followed the crowd towards the exit. "Kinda," I admitted. "I'm going to be the photographer for their Santa."

Sadie squeezed my elbow and I wasn't sure if it was out of support or the fear of being separated as the crowd bottlenecked at the door. "Great!" she exclaimed supportively. "You're welcome to spend the night at my apartment so you don't have to walk through all the snow on Oak Street," she offered.

"Yeah, maybe," I said, picturing myself in her bright, French- and sunflower-themed apartment, smack dab in the middle of downtown Alton Oaks. At the moment, I still preferred my dark and out-dated bedroom at the Alton House.

Chapter Three

THE CLOSER THE CALENDAR CREPT toward Christmas, the more indifferent I felt. I was directionless, unless I was behind my camera. I held onto that device like a life jacket, carrying it with me everywhere. It was my anchor to reality; a tether to the memory of who I used to be. Even when Sadie dropped me off at the Alton House, I fell into my bed still gripping my camera case.

I really wasn't trying to intentionally be dramatic. When I'd come back to Alton Oaks in April, I'd pushed away my feelings instead of working through them. I thought there would be time; time to confront Jackson, time to get closure, time to mourn my marriage before we signed divorce papers. No, I shoved it all away until Jackson's death, when it started seeping out in uncontrolled bursts, like when you unkink the garden hose and the water comes out in full force, before it kinks again or someone steps on it. One kink after another released a burst of emotion and I just wished it would all come pouring out so I could get on with my life.

"You sure you don't want to pick up a shift tonight?" Dad asked as he poked his head into my bedroom.

He repeatedly offered me a shift as hostess, waitress,

dishwasher, whatever, at Oakie's Bar & Grill, where he was the manager. "No," I said, stifling a yawn. I knew the college kids were home for the holidays and he didn't need me anyway. "I'm starting at Oakie Doughkie tomorrow."

"Ah, that's right," he said and gingerly sat at the foot of my bed. His reindeer-themed necktie lit up Rudolph's nose when he pressed the secret button. It was loose around his neck. "Maybe we should get a family picture this year," he said, and added, "since we're altogether."

Internally, I winced. I hadn't been home for Christmas in two years—Jackson and I'd just had to take that ski vacation last year where he'd ditched me—his story of "getting lost" was probably a cover for "running into Jessica" on our three night stay. I felt a kink coming loose and nodded. "Sounds great, Dad, but who'll take the picture?" I asked.

Dad hit the secret button and his tie lit up. A small but genuine smile crossed my lips. "I love you, Dad," I said.

He pulled me into a hug, sitting on my mattress. "Love you too, Charlotte May I." His nickname for me always made me feel safe and secure, like home should feel.

I relished in the hug for a bit longer than normal. I breathed in the scent of soap with a faint hint of Oakie's deep-fried chicken as I listened to his nickname for me echo in my head. I wanted time to stand still; for him not to go to work, to hold me like he did when I woke up in the middle of the night from a bad dream as a six-year-old. But I was twenty-eight-years old. An adult. Married. No, *widowed*.

"Have a good day," I said, noting the sunlight seeping in from behind my bedroom curtains.

I watched his shadow in the hallway get longer until he descended the stairs. The alarm clock beside my bed read noon; its red light illuminated the dust that collected on the top; the only disturbance was the swipe that cut through on the snooze button.

Mom had left a note for me this morning on the fridge, hinting that they could use an extra hand at the library today for children's story time at 1:30. Both of my parents had been passive about my lack of direction, especially since Jackson's death. They could tell I was going through grief, but didn't directly try to help me, or get flustered that I was sleeping in their house and eating their food at no charge... well, at least they didn't say anything to my face.

But I felt guilty. I felt lost, wishing there was a roadmap to my life within reach. And now, worst of all, I felt unmotivated. Sometimes I wished my father would force me to take a shift at the restaurant or that my mother would make me sign a lease where I paid rent. At least then I could feel like I was contributing to society. But it was my problem and my life. I needed to figure out what to do next. What did I want out of life? What made me happy?

I don't have to figure it out now, I told myself as my head hit the pillow, already exhausted. I stared at the papasan chair in the corner, covered in dirty clothes, as I gave into the dark, crushing grip of depression once more.

The sun set around four o'clock and when my eyes opened again, I had to make sure the clock wasn't referring to five-thirty in the morning. Besides Sadie's sporadic adventures that dragged me out of my room— when her work schedule allowed it—I only found the motivation to get dressed and brave the cold on the other side of my blanket when I had the urge to take pictures for *The Oak Leaf Press*. The great thing about Alton Oaks in

December is that there was no shortage of photographic opportunities.

The old mattress springs screeched as I sat on the edge of the bed and pulled on a pair of wool socks. I realized that I'd have to start work as a professional photographer tomorrow at the Oakie Doughkie Bakery and Gift Shop. I had mixed feelings about it because I wasn't a professional photographer. I felt like this was one of those events in life that could change the course of my lifetime and I really didn't want to mess it up. Of course, I was probably being a worry-wort and subconsciously trying to fail at it.

Nevertheless, I fretted over the to-do list in my head. I became fatigued just thinking about the tasks: I had to clean and restock my camera bag, set up the printer, put together some lighting solutions, find my gray card, and download the updates to my photo editing software— which was a lot of fun to use, but an expensive purchase.

Last Tuesday, after the cookie-decorating excursion, I'd tagged along with Bailey to Davenport where I bought an external memory port, a heavy-duty photo printer, and stocked up on ink while my sister went Christmas shopping for Eli. The money I'd earned working as the hospital's Special Event Coordinator & Project Manager for the Spooktacular Spook Show and Boo Ball and also being the Project Developer for the Dee Dempsey Greenhouse & Outdoor Education and Play Area for the Alton Oaks school district had taken a huge dent. I looked at the pile of purchases on my desk, still in their manufacturer boxes and plastic yellow and black shopping bags, knowing I had to put them together and figure out how they worked by morning. My shoulders slumped and I longed to lie back down on my pillow.

"Charli! Are you here?" I heard Sadie's voice from the

first floor of the Alton House. The wind howled outside my bedroom window as I laced up my snow boots.

"Yeah!" I yelled, hoping I could hitch a ride with her to town. My voice cracked and I cleared my throat. Besides the exchange between my father and me, it was the first word I'd uttered all day, despite wanting to yell at Rip—Alton Oaks' handyman extraordinaire—who was making too much noise this morning as he continued to work on fixing the dilapidated north end of our historical family home.

He'd contracted professionals to install a new roof before the first snow fell. Now he'd employed "interns" from the local high school and was working on patching the holes in the floor of the loft, not too far from my bedroom door. "I'll be down in a minute!" I shouted and moved about my bedroom to grab all the layers of clothes I'd need to keep warm.

The town's Tree Lighting Ceremony was in about an hour and I hoped to get a few pictures for the newspaper. I grabbed my thin but warm leather gloves and slung the strap of my camera case on my shoulder before I left the bedroom. A gentle blue glow from the dusk and snow illuminated the shadows of the hallway as the floorboards creaked with my weight.

To my delight, both Sadie and my brother Alex were waiting at the bottom of the staircase. Their boots still dripped with snow on the rug in the foyer. Despite the rubbery squeak my boots made on the aged floor boards, they hadn't noticed me. I stopped for a second and let them have a moment as my heart swelled for them. They were my two favorite people in the world and despite growing up together, they were so lucky to have found each other.

I watched as Sadie looked up at Alex with a smile. Her

dark auburn hair swept across her shoulders with the movement, while the creamy white wool beret stayed in place on her head. And despite Alex recently getting a haircut, his brown hair was still messy and unruly, just like my dad's. His glasses slipped down his nose as he looked at Sadie and one of his gloved hands moved to fix them.

"Alex!" I exclaimed, bounding down the stairs, "I thought you were working!" I enveloped him and his chilled pea coat as soon as I reached the foyer. My brother was a doctor at St. Colette's hospital, so it was no wonder he and Sadie—a pediatric nurse there—eventually found each other.

"Hey, Charli May," he greeted and rubbed my head in a half-hearted noogie as I pulled away. "I just got off the clock," he admitted as I noticed exhaustion tugging at the corners of his eyes.

"We brought you an early Christmas present," Sadie said, her eyes bright with enthusiasm. She gestured to her right where a large box, draped with a reindeer-and-snowman themed blanket, leaned against the dining room table.

A smile crept across my face and I didn't even have to try. Knowing Sadie, it was probably a build-your-own-indoor snowman kit or a hideously hilarious lawn decoration. Without a word, I tugged on the blanket, letting the fringe on the end tickle my wrist. Tears tickled my throat when I realized that it wasn't a gag gift or a silly present. "You guys," I said, tripping over the lump in my throat. I knelt down to inspect the contents of the box marked Photo & Video Studio Kit.

"It's not the high-grade professional photographer stuff," Sadie admitted, "but it'll get you started."

"A light stand? A white and black umbrella reflector? A

soft box?" I exclaimed, beside myself, gripping the large box as if it would be taken away from me at any moment. These were tools that real photographers had; I couldn't wait to experiment with them!

"It comes with a carrying case," Sadie added, pointing to the picture on the box.

"I can help you set up tomorrow morning before my next shift," Alex offered. "We thought this might help out with the gig at the bakery."

I'd been feeling so down and depressed lately that this gesture was a ray of sunlight in my gloomy world. "Thanks, you guys," I said genuinely, pulling them both into a hug with glassy eyes. "Thank you," I repeated as I smelled a hint of fabric softener from Alex's ear-warmers and the melted snowflakes had exaggerated the scent of Sadie's shampoo. I realized that it wasn't so much the gesture that made me emotional, but their support and encouragement of my hobby.

"It's not a problem, Charli May," Alex said after I pulled away and tried not to let tears fall in front of them—it seemed like that was a full time job lately.

"Come on," Sadie said, linking her arm around my elbow. "We can tear into this later tonight. Let's head out to the tree decorating! I want to get my hands on some of those roasted chestnuts before they're sold out!"

Pulling myself away from my new gift, I nodded. My soul felt lighter as I pulled my heavy black down coat from the hall closet. I didn't want to think about how long this little high would last, because then a countdown to the tearful nights in bed would start. Sadie and Alex were a good distraction. I grabbed my camera bag and followed them out the door.

Alton Oaks is a small town, usually brimming with a

lot of tourists. Normally, most of the Canaries—our local term for out-of-towners—flocked in throughout the spring and summer to ride the Whett River Canal Trail, participate in the annual bicycle race in the spring, celebrate Founder's Day in the summer, or partake in a variety of our fall attractions like the Parade of Scarecrows or the Boo Ball. However, the Tree Lighting ceremony in Alton Oaks' Town Circle drew a majority of the town and citizens from Sheridan, Terryville—even Sandalwood! I'd forgotten about how big this event was until we hit a traffic jam before we even made it to Main Street. As soon as possible, Alex turned down Sheridan Avenue and made the rough and bumpy trek down Blackhill Avenue. It hadn't been plowed, but instead packed down by large four-wheel trucks that usually only traveled between the Miller's Farm and US-16.

I held onto the leather interior of his Jeep, hoping we wouldn't get stuck in the snow, until we pulled into his garage off First Street West. "Well, ladies," he said, putting the vehicle in park in his dimly lit garage, "it looks like we're walking from here."

When you look at a map of Alton Oaks, it wasn't that far of a walk—maybe twenty minutes. But if you're looking at the current weather conditions in Alton Oaks, it seemed like a long walk. Our local Public Works Department always does a great job at plowing and snow removal downtown. Our perfectly paved sidewalks were always clear and sprinkled with salt to deter ice from forming. The problem was the cold wind scraping across our faces as it dragged its icy fingernails down the street. However, as we passed the families walking up the road, bundled in layers of snow gear, they were all smiles; the children ran ahead and kicked the piles of snow with jubilance. Even Sadie was glowing.

"Last year The Buzz had their van on the fairgrounds and were selling the best caramel apple cider," Sadie explained, her chin dipping in and out of the black and white plaid blanket scarf around her neck. "Oh! And the high school did a super awesome performance from their winter show—they had singing and dancing and tumbling... I hope they do it again!" she mused as we made our way to Oak & Main.

I caught the smile that my brother gave Sadie, though she didn't. Alex had had a serious girlfriend in high school and another in college, but I never saw him look at either the way he looked at Sadie. Their happiness warmed my heart, but also stung it as I was reminded of happier days with Jackson.

In the distance, just the other side of Maple Lane, stood Town Circle, with the frozen Whett River in the background. The public buildings—town hall, the court house, the visitor's center, parks & recreation, and public works—were triangle slices that made up the circle with a large Christmas tree in the middle. As we passed the holly and twinkle lights wrapped around the pillars of town hall and the green and red lights that made the court house steps festively glow, we could see the smaller Christmas trees surrounding it. It's been a tradition for citizens to "purchase" a young tree that stood in Town Circle and they could decorate it any way they wanted. Usually it was in memory of someone who'd passed or to represent an organization or club. The trees remained decorated until all the town's holiday decorations came down on January seventh.

The crowd became thicker as we approached the main event. Many people had parked on the fairgrounds just to the west of the gardens and walked over the muddy paths. My heart soared as we passed a tree that was loaded with decorations, pictures, and ornaments. Wrapped around the trunk was a simple yet beautiful sign in wispy letters: In Memory of Ms. Dee Dempsey. She was the teacher who'd been murdered over the summer and I'd been wrongfully accused of the crime. She was loved and continued to change children's lives after her demise. Her fiance, Lyle, adjusted his tortoise shell spectacles with a gloved hand as he nodded a greeting in my direction. One could tell by the passing students adding an ornament, and by the children playing in the Dee Dempsey Outdoor Education & Play Area to the east of Town Circle, that she was not only loved, but made a difference in many lives of this generation.

The sound of the high school Madrigals, dressed in period attire, were singing Good King Wenceslas beside the yet-to-be-lit tree with enthusiasm and grace. Wooden stable-like booths were erected on the outskirts of the crowd—along the circle between the buildings and the gardens—where local businesses and artists set up their own Chriskindle Market. Tendrils of steam climbed out of the cardboard cups coming from The Buzz's station, and happy children with half-eaten sugar cookies skipped away from Oakie Doughkie's booth.

Just past the gardens, along the Whett River Canal Trail, I knew there would be metal barrels of fiery coals that roasted chestnuts and popcorn, and—if the Cut It Out butcher shop was still on Main Street—smoked meats and jerky.

"Oh look!" Sadie said, pointing to the town's library booth. I followed her gloved hand and saw my sister's family looking Christmas-card perfect in front of it. "Let's go say hi to your mom," she urged, walking towards the booth without waiting for my brother or me to answer.

Alex and I exchanged glances—we both could only

stand our little sister for so long. As we got closer, though, I noticed that the free candy-canes had lured Sadie in, not my sister's company. "Oh, hi, Bailey," Sadie greeted awkwardly, as if she'd been a bug lured into the porch light and realized she'd passed the point of no return.

Bailey turned her knee-high black boots away from her family and gave a warm smile. "Hi, Sadie," my sister greeted. Her pink cheeks accented her blue eyes and frizz-free pale blonde hair as she pulled Sadie into a hug. Alex and I stifled a laugh as Sadie reached for a free candy cane, behind my sister's back.

"Are you all writing a letter to Santa, too?" Bailey asked when she saw Alex and me walk up behind Sadie.

My mother approached the booth, behind the women who wore lit up Santa hats. She carried a cardboard box and moaned a bit when she let it fall onto the green metal folding chair. "These should be enough envelopes," she informed, her warm breath billowing into the night air.

"Oh, all my babies are here!" she lit up, without a novelty hat, at the sight of her three children within ten feet of each other—and it wasn't even a holiday (yet). "Eli, honey, are you writing a letter to Santa?" my mother asked, her attention immediately turning to her one and only grandchild.

"Yep," he answered. It suddenly struck me how much my nephew had grown. He must recently have had a growth spurt because he was now well past my hips and had only inches before he reached Sadie's shoulder. I noticed her standing up a bit straighter as she slipped him a candy cane from the bowl with a wink. "I want a rock climbing wall for the backyard with a trampoline!" he announced with pride.

"My, that's a tall order for Santa," the woman beside my mother said, surprised. "Why not a football or a video game?"

"I like to watch my Mom's face when Daddy and I climb the rocks at The Cove," he admitted with a giggle and I couldn't help but laugh too.

Bailey shot her husband Carter a look, but he'd been too busy devouring what looked like a roasted turkey leg. Mid-bite, he gave Bailey a you-can't-help-but-love-me smile. I might not always get along with my little sister, but she'd made a good choice when she let Carter hold her hand in sixth grade, walking her home from school. They'd been happily together, for the most part, ever since.

sighed. As my mother roped Sadie and Alex into writing a Christmas card for the troops, I slipped into the crowd and took out my camera.

Slinging the camera strap around my neck and lifting the weight of the device to my eye, I suddenly felt at ease; like the moment you slip off that pair of high heel shoes and trade them in for the most comfortable fuzzy pair of slippers.

Snap, snap, snap. I could never get tired of the sound of the shutter. I captured the crowd from the back—down on Maple Street where the buildings glowed with light and excitement. I captured them from above on the podium beside the dark tree where people snuck hopeful glances at the possibilities that lie within the darkness. The brightly lit cross above the church in Moss Cove, the village on just the other side of the Whett River, reflected on the ice in the background of the holiday chaos.

There was a picture of a garden troll drawn by a talented child hanging from Ms. Dempsey's Tree with #1 Teacher and Best Teacher Ever ornaments along with thank you notes that hung with glitter and construction paper in the background. Beyond, parents lifted up their children so they could mail their letter to Santa in the large faux red mail box beside the library booth, and children in colorful scarves climbed into the present-filled sleigh, posing for a photo on their parent's cell phone.

Happy customers ate elaborately decorated sugar cookies from the Oakie Doughkie bakery and warm, loaded cheese fries or mouthwatering Swedish meatballs from Oakie's booth. And a large glass bowl that collected the money for the St. Collette's raffle—two free tickets to the Holiday Hop—reflected the crowd of hopeful people wishing for a ticket to the hottest event in the county.

Just outside town circle, Mrs. Kratsky straddled a snow mobile—her golf cart was stored in the garage until the snow and mud of winter was gone. Dismounting, she stood beside her husband and Father McKinsley, laughing at an unheard joke. She waved her thickly insulated leather mittens in my direction. I lowered the camera for a moment to wave.

"Char-berry!" a voice called out from a few yards behind me. I let the warmth of her greeting and term of endearment spread through my limbs.

"Jilly Bean!" I greeted, already expecting a hug from my favorite cousin. Jillian—and her twin sister Jenna— were ten years my senior. Growing up, Jenna and Bailey had taken a liking to each other—even with the fourteen year age gap. I think Jenna was preparing to be a Mom, and when she found out that she and her husband couldn't conceive, she began spoiling Bailey as if she were her own. Jillian had been my baby-sitter and a pseudo-older sister: letting me borrow her clothes and be the annoying kid who hung out with her and her friends.

The smell of patchouli and frankincense clung to her aura. I noticed that she was in pressed black pants beneath her long red pea coat, drastically different from her hemp and cotton-made outfits or yoga clothes that I'd catch her in at home. "Just coming from work?" I asked.

Jillian was a paralegal at Westbrook Attorneys just a block away. She'd been a big help when I was accused of murdering Ms. Dempsey and when trying to sort out the details of Jackson's death. Luckily, the law office represented me when Jackson's parents came to town and I didn't have to see them. They were currently working on the debt Jackson had accumulated when I left town— since he and I were still technically married—and the status of his questionable accounts in the Cayman Islands.

"Yeah," Jillian said, tucking her side bangs—a new style I really liked—behind her ears. They popped back onto her face which released a tinge of annoyance across her features. The light of the nearby festive lights illuminated the scar on her right temple. "Dad wanted me to come out for a bit," she divulged.

My Uncle Randy—Jillian's father—was the mayor of Alton Oaks. His wife had died when I was a child, and my only real memory of her was that she wouldn't let her kids eat sugar. "Is Jenna here too?" I asked, scanning the crowd on my tip-toes.

"I suppose," she said and sighed. "What's this I hear about you being a professional photographer?" Jillian asked, nudging me with her elbow. "You've surpassed the likes of *The Oak Leaf Press*?"

"Man," I said with shock. It still blows my mind how fast gossip spread in this small town. "How did you hear?"

Jillian shrugged. "Jenna. I'm assuming she either heard it from Bailey or Aunt Rose." She passed it off like the information wasn't important. "So?" she urged, her bright blue eyes prodded for details.

Before I could explain my new job opportunity, the feedback on the microphone squealed, turning everyone's attention to the podium beside the large, dark, pine tree. "Good evening, fellow citizens of Alton Oaks, and a warm welcome to visitors," my uncle's voice was soothing but firm as it filled the Town Circle. His dark hair was cut short and peppered heavily in gray; his smooth features gave way to more wrinkles as each year passed.

The crowd moved in, pushing Jillian and me closer to the gap between the courthouse and the public works building. As my uncle thanked sponsors and made a lengthy announcement about the coveted Holiday Hop raffle, I couldn't help but notice a young couple—probably still in high school—in front of us. The girl's curly red hair was held back in two French braids that peeked out from beneath her stocking cap. Her light brown coat looked warm with fleece lining in the inside of the hood that she chose not to lift onto her head. The boy's shoulder leaned into the girl as if the contact of his thin black coat was all she needed and wanted at the moment; that that one point of contact kept them connected more resolutely than any handhold or hug could.

I was so lost in their world that I didn't notice the countdown that echoed among the crowd. When the tree was lit and bathed Town Circle in its festive glow, the girl leaned her head on the boy's shoulder and I couldn't help but take a picture: their silhouettes against the tree lights.

When Santa came to the podium to make his jolly announcements about photographs at the bakery, my attention was brought back to the young couple. An older gentleman—possibly the girl's father—angrily pulled the red-haired girl from beside the boy.

"Dad!" she whispered in shock as they exited the crowd beside the courthouse. She put her hand over his as he gripped her wrist, as if to cover up the act. She looked around, hoping to avoid a scene.

"Madeline," his voice was deep and menacing, but he kept the tone lower than expected. "I've told you several times," he started, pulling her between the two buildings. He tugged on her so that she bumped into his broad, flannel-clad arms more than once.

"Daddy, please," her voice was pleading. "I just wanted to see the tree lighting like a normal teenager." The flood lights from the gardens crept over the public works building and elongated their shadows onto the courthouse wall. I itched to take a picture of how tragic the scene looked against the red, green, and blue lights.

For a moment I thought he was going to give her a high five with the way he raised his hand, which puzzled me. Then he lowered it, slowly, as if he realized it wasn't a normal action. "Go," he said with force. "Get in the car. We'll continue this when we get home."

I watched their shadows disappear as they walked deeper between the buildings. "I guess someone was caught sneaking out with a boy," Jillian mused under her breath.

My attention went back to the boy in black whose eyes didn't leave the space between the buildings. His burning gaze, tense shoulders and measured breaths gave me shivers. Anger wasn't even the term I'd use to describe him—overwrought or vengeful would be more appropriate.

"Yeah," I said, half-agreeing with Jillian.

The boy disappeared down the same pathway with determined and agitated footsteps. I was suddenly extremely thankful that I had my dad and not someone else's.

Chapter Four

"OKAY, LOOK RIGHT HERE!" I said, waving a large yellow duck that squeaked when I pressed its belly. I pressed the shutter button on my camera just as the fifteen-month-old smiled in her frilly white and red velvet dress.

"Oh it's wonderful!" Tabitha said, bending down to look at my computer screen. I had gone to high school with her, but neither of us mentioned it in this exchange.

I looked at the computer screen and felt relieved that, after twenty minutes of fussing over the tiny child, we finally got her to stop crying. "How many copies can I get?" Tabitha asked, picking up the child from Santa's lap.

Pointing to the sign the Oakie Doughkie Bakery had printed and posted on the wall, I went over the pricing packages. Honestly, I was a bit upset that they were getting 40% of each transaction and at these prices. I wouldn't break even with the supplies I'd purchased. Taking a deep breath, I let it go and wondered if it was possible to place a tip jar at my station. I guess one perk was the enticing scent of freshly baked bread in the morning and sweet, just-out-of-the-oven cookies all day.

My stomach rumbled as I printed the biggest package for Tabitha as she put her child back in her snow suit and secured her in the stroller, soothing her with a bottle. Though the clock above the cash register didn't quite read three o'clock, I seriously contemplated another cup of coffee.

"Thank you so much for coming," I said in my faux, happy-that-you're-here, customer service voice as I handed her the package of photographs in a Manila envelope. "Here's a coupon, good until the end of the month. When you're ready, Mrs. Prince will check you out," I instructed, nodding to the woman with tired ginger hair behind the counter.

Luckily, it was a slow opening day. There had been a steady flow of customers at noon, when Santa officially took the floor, but not many since. I hadn't been in the gift shop before today, and was pleasantly surprised when Alex, Sadie, and I dragged my supplies in early in the morning. The smell of freshly baked cinnamon rolls had already permeated the air and, mixed with our to-go cups of The Buzz's strongest coffee, it made for a pleasant morning—even as I swore under my breath when I couldn't get the camera to communicate with the laptop or printer.

There used to be a wall that separated the bakery from the store beside it, but half of it had been torn down so that it opened into the gift shop. The front door was decorated in a 11" x 14", candy-cane border poster that advertised the hours for Meet Santa this coming week. If that didn't draw people in, then the smell of warm gingerbread cookies and the elaborate three-tier gingerbread house in the display window would! Next to the no-nonsense, black and white, block-lettered menus with precise prices ($1.18 per doughnut!) was an advertisement with brightly-colored clip art giving the dates and prices for classes in cake-decorating, basic baking, build-your-own-gingerbread house, and an all-call for volunteers to help bake cookies for the Snow Social at the children's hospital.

While the bakery was lacking decoration (except the snowman-themed tinsel-garland at the register, the candy-cane-shaped pen for signing receipts and the holiday treats in the display case), the gift shop was bursting with holiday cheer. Not only were they selling mugs ("Coffee puts me on the Nice List"), decorative signs ("Merry Memories Made Here"), and apparel (shirts and hats donning a red and white Santa Hat on the A of Alton and a snowman made of the O in Oaks), and holiday music wafted from the radio behind the glass counter of snow globes and timepieces.

I avoided looking at Santa as I sat down at the two rickety TV trays covered in scraps of holiday fabric where my computer and printer rested. He sat in the corner, in an old loveseat amongst fake snow, a ribbon-happy Christmas tree, and cardboard boxes wrapped in brightly colored wrapping paper. He was played by Mr. Robinson, who I'm sure had been grumpy since the day he was born. Instead, I looked at my tripod, camera, and light umbrella, proud of how professional it looked. "Can ya get that light out of my face?" Santa grumbled. He took off the red and white hat and scratched his nearly bald head.

"Yeah, sorry," I said, getting up and flipping the switch that turned out the bright light. I couldn't quite figure out how to hook it up so that it only flashed when I took a pictures. Alex left long before I needed to troubleshoot that.

There were no customers in the store and I twirled my thumbs, reading the t-shirts, mugs, and signs on display around me. "How are things working out?" Mrs. Robinson asked as she came around the corner in her brown and pink apron.

"Oh, just fine," I said. "Thanks again for this job."

"Sophia," Mr. Robinson grunted as he stood up from the sofa. "I'm going on break. Every year I forget how itchy this suit is and there's a rash this time," he said, pulling up his sleeve.

"Oh dear," Mrs. Robinson remarked, gripping her left thumb and wringing it with her opposite hand. "I'll remember to lay out your—" she called after him as he disappeared through the back door without acknowledging her. Her sentence was cut off by the slamming of the back door, its glass rattling in the wake of Mr. Robinson's irritation.

When her attention drifted back to me, she said, "Thanks for being the photographer. My husband didn't want to hire a real photography studio. You know, small business and everything." She put her hands in the pocket of her apron and sighed while I tried not to take offense to her comment.

"I know it's not very busy right now," she admitted. "It'll pick up after dinner." I glanced at my wristwatch just in time to hear the dismissal bell at the school a block away. "You have about forty-five minutes until Mr. Robinson gets back. Make sure you eat because from about four-thirty to eight o'clock, there should be a steady flow of customers."

I nodded and moved to grab my water bottle beneath the tray table as Mrs. Robinson disappeared into the bakery. Looking over my equipment once more, I decided to unplug the wires from my camera and take it with me.

"Also," Mrs. Robinson called over the counter as I opened the door to the wintry weather. "Be ready tomorrow morning. If history repeats itself, as it tends to do, there will be a line out the door, so hopefully there won't be any quirks with your equipment."

With a half-hearted smile in response, I ventured out into the blistering winter that jostled the snowflakes retiring on the window ledges and awnings of the surrounding buildings.

It was hard to get in the holiday mood this year. This coming from the girl who had her two-foot Christmas tree and collection of dollar store and clearance-purchased decorations up and out of storage on Thanksgiving night. Even when I returned to the store—after pacing the streets of downtown Alton Oaks for half an hour—the candy cane tiara I was given to wear only irritated me as it kept falling when I looked into my camera.

After several steady hours of customers, I noted that I'd have to overnight a lot more glossy picture paper if the weekend would be twice as busy. Mariah Carey's iconic holiday song was streaming throughout the store as Mrs. Lupizo exited with her grandchildren and a newly framed 8" x 10" picture of them in their matching snowmen-themed pajamas on Santa's lap. I had become immune to the intoxicating scent of baked goods and when the heat kicked on, the scent of nearby balsam fir and peppermint scented candles crossed my path. If it wasn't for grumpy Mr. Robinson in his itchy Santa suit, this gig wouldn't have been half bad.

I sat on the folding chair in the empty store, stealing a moment to catch up on emailing the photos I'd taken today to paying customers. As I scrolled through the folder of tears, smiles, and awkward emotions from confused children, I sighed. I remembered when Chief Gomes dressed up as Santa for the church when we were younger and my mother always got a picture of Alex, Bailey, and me with him. She made them into ornaments that hung on our tree each year. I was convinced that

Santa watched us all year round, disguised as a policeman, as if he was a secret agent spy. I'd been impressed by him from the start.

The bell on the door to the bakery jingled and I automatically minimized the window to my email in order to greet a potential customer. I was mildly surprised to see the red-headed girl from last night's tree lighting ceremony enter, bundled up in a green knit hat with matching scarf which made her look very Irish. "Hi, Grandma," she said with a tired smile, waving her hand to Mrs. Robinson behind the counter.

"Hi, sweetie," Mrs. Robinson returned the greeting, and grabbing a tray from the table behind her. "Have something to eat," she urged. When my grandpa died, long before I was born, my grandmother moved to Sandalwood and she always had a candy dish on the table in the living room for us. The gesture I witnessed reminded me so much of my childhood.

"I can't, grandma," the girl said reluctantly. "I haven't had dinner."

The girl glanced towards the gift shop where Ruby was hunched over the counter with a notebook and calculator. The bags under her eyes were as evident as her cotton candy-like, tired ginger hair.

"My dear girl," Mrs. Robinson started, leaning over the counter with a tray of cookies. "How many times do I have to tell you? I'm grandma and I trump both your parents when it comes to treats."

The young girl's lips pulled into a tight smile as she reached for a cookie, but her tense shoulders never did relax. Instead, she devoured the cookie in two bites and then made her way to the counter where Ruby sat, loosening the scarf around her neck.

"Hi, Mama," she greeted without much warmth. She

pulled off her jacket and hung it on the coat rack behind the partition. She went through the motions of tying a red apron around her waist and placing a festive headband—complete with light-up, plush, Christmas trees as antennae—on her head with a bit of amusement in her features.

"Hi baby," Ruby greeted without looking up. "Would you mind closing the store for me? I need to finish this before the end of the month. I'll just be in the back room." It was never meant to be a question, but a polite demand.

"Yes, Mama," the girl replied obediently.

Ruby didn't waste a second compiling her work and retreating behind the "Employees Only" door beside the Oakie Doughkie counter. I could hear the snores of Mr. Robinson twenty feet in front of me and felt relief. As long as there were no customers in the store, I hoped the other women would let him sleep so as to avoid his complaining.

The young girl hoisted a cardboard box from beneath the counter and began placing the items inside back onto the shelves. When she came near me to replace a Christmas-themed Alton Oaks t-shirt and straighten the pile, I interrupted her thoughts, throwing her off guard. "Can I help with anything?" I asked.

Looking a bit like she was cornered in a dangerous alley, she soon gathered her senses. "Sorry, I didn't know you were there," she replied and her cheeks turned pink.

"I didn't mean to scare you," I said, standing up from my folding chair. The girl was so short that I felt like a giant beside her. Instinctively, I took a few steps back so the difference wasn't as apparent. "I'm Charli," I said.

"I'm Maddie," she said meekly, sneaking glances at her snoozing grandfather.

"Are you in high school?" I guessed, based on what I

saw last night.

Maddie nodded as she folded the t-shirts. "Senior," she informed, which surprised me.

I thought back to my senior year at Riley C. Shepard High School. The students of Terryville, Alton Oaks, and Sheridan commuted and shared that school. I'd spent too much time there, physically and mentally, the past two months as it was the last place I'd seen my husband alive. "Are you thinking about college?" I asked, pushing aside the wave of emotions that threatened to overcome me.

Maddie shrugged without answering my question. The sleeve of her long white turtleneck had left her wrist exposed and I noticed a bruise around it. She quickly pulled on her sleeve and stumbled over her words, "I'm sorry. I need to finish this stuff before we close."

I watched as she picked the box up and scurried over to the opposite side of the store. I never caught her glancing in my direction as she straightened up the small shelf of books or as she restocked the postcard rack. When she'd finished her tasks, she spent the last ten minutes with her nose in a school book, hunched over the counter like her mother.

When the plain black-and-white, no-nonsense clock on the wall hit the hour, Mr. Robinson was still snoozing on set. Without worrying about him, I packed up my camera and laptop and turned off the printer and power to the lighting. "Bye, Maddie; it was nice meeting you," I said as I walked past her, adjusting the backpack straps on my shoulders, looking for eye contact.

"Bye, Charli," she said, barely lifting her eyes from the book.

The little bell above the door signaled my exit and before I even left the front sidewalk, Maddie had locked the door and turned off the display lights. I couldn't put my finger on why our exchange was so awkward, and I didn't care to give enough energy towards figuring it out. A blast of cold air raced down the street and I could taste snow in the air; it would come tonight while the town slept.

Chapter Five

IT WOULD TAKE ME OVER FORTY-FIVE minutes to get home in this weather. I glanced at the library and noticed that the Winter Reading Lock-In was in session—students and scouts spending the night in the library to kick off their winter reading list. My mom had been prepping for it the past two weeks; they play movies based on books in the media room, there's a read aloud marathon in the tween meeting room, and an award for the most pages read that night. If my mother caught a glimpse of me, she'd unlock the door in a heartbeat and recruit me to be a chaperone.

I contemplated the ten minute walk to Sadie's apartment and hunkering down there for the night. To my pleasant surprise, however, I ran into Rip as he was exiting the art gallery next door. As usual, the force of me running into him didn't seem to faze him.

"You're a walking disaster waiting to happen," he commented in greeting. When Rip had moved to Alton Oaks this spring, we'd gotten off on the wrong foot. Now, however, I considered us friends despite the jabs we constantly exchanged.

"North Pole University, huh?" I inquired, pointing to the festive baseball cap on his head. "Surprised they let you in."

Rip put his hands in the pockets of his puffer coat and rolled his eyes. "I excelled in both shenanigans and tomfoolery," he commented in good humor.

"That explains the hat," I said as we walked down Main Street together, battling the wind.

"I find I get more business if I take part in these festive town things," he explained. "Candy cane?" he asked, pulling one out of his pocket.

"Who are you?" I asked, taken aback by his play-along demeanor, and still grabbing the candy cane from his fist.

Another gust of wind barreled down the street and tore the hood of the parka off my head. "Heading home?" Rip asked as I replaced my hood with a gloved hand. I nodded.

"Want a ride?" Rip offered as he turned the corner on Oak Street and I saw his black pick-up truck parked along the curb. He'd already put his motorcycle away for the winter, much to the relief of Mrs. Watson who was constantly calling the police station with a noise complaint.

"Who are you?" I asked again, dumbfounded at his uncharacteristic behavior. Normally, Rip would've let me walk up Oak Street and pulled over when he saw me somewhere between First and Second Street battling the icy patches. He either liked to have that control or be seen as the rescuer.

Climbing into his truck, I felt my cheeks grow warm with wind burn, but thankful to be out of the thick of it. Heat poured from the radiator vents and I put my gloved hands in front of them.

A few weeks ago, I'd taken Rip's truck to the mechanic shop in Terryville and had them replace the passenger side mirror and the tailgate door. They'd been damaged with bullet holes because of me in October, when I thought my

life would end in this truck. I still couldn't shake that
uneasy feeling when I climbed into the cabin. It made me
wonder where Jesse and Sean ended up. Were the rumors
about Witness Protection true?

"Enjoying the artist's life?" Rip asked and nodded to
the backpack of supplies I'd tucked on the floor between
my feet.

In typical Rip fashion, he hit the gas pedal and
exploded up the road while I tested my seatbelt's security.
"Livin' the dream," I said, sarcastically. "What were you
doing at the art gallery?"

"Securing brackets for a new display. Doing work at
the Alton House has been lucrative for business," Rip
commented, referring to his 'Handyman Extraordinaire'
business.

My parent's house was built by my great-great
grandfather who founded our town. Needless to say, the
house was old and needed a lot care of TLC. When it
became an Illinois Historic Landmark, the town secured a
grant to fix it up to preserve its historic glory. My mother
was swayed by her brother—the mayor—to keep the
business local and grudgingly hired the new guy in town
that she wasn't a big fan of—and I'm still not sure why
she harbored those feelings. I chalked it up to Rip being a
rough-around-the-edges, city-boy in my mom's small
town.

"I'll have to thank her for that one day," Rip mused as
we sped past the junior high school.

"Who are you?" I asked yet again. Rip didn't trust my
mother, and the feeling was pretty mutual.

Rip sighed. "A man with a booming business,
currently," he admitted. "Are you working all weekend?"
he asked before I could make a sarcastic comment.

"Yep," I remarked, not looking forward to it. I loved

photography, but I wasn't a fan of the mass-marketing photography this job seemed to be... and dealing with people (especially Mr. Robinson). Still, it was a paycheck and it got me out of bed each day.

"Oh," he said, sounding surprised. "I thought you'd be at the Polar Plunge tomorrow."

"No, I will be," I corrected. "I'm taking pictures for *The Oak Leaf Press* and then heading to the store." I wondered how being an hour late past the regular photography schedule would affect Mr. Robinson's attitude, despite this stipulation being ironed out between Mrs. Robinson and me before I started. I didn't look forward to dealing with him any day, especially when he had something to hold over me.

"I'll see you there, then," he said as he pulled onto the gravel, unpaved road on our side of town.

This confused me because Rip didn't like partaking in the town's activities. I still remember how he scoffed at the Fall Fest, the giant planted acorns around town, and the Trail of Scarecrows. Before I could ask, *Who are you?* again, he asked, "Are you participating?"

"In the polar plunge?" I asked incredulously. Shivers ran up and down my spine just thinking about a bare toe touching the freezing water of the Whett River.

"Yeah," he said. The truck skid slightly on the unpaved, icy road as we neared his house. "I did it when I was living in Norway. *Nieuwjaarduik* is a tradition on New Year's there. It's supposed to be good for you, good for your health."

That man never stopped being an enigma. I looked at him dumbfounded as he pulled into his driveway. "You know there's an entrance fee, right? It's to raise money for the hospital," I shared.

"Yeah," he said, putting the car into park beside his

house. "I read about the fundraiser in the newspaper. I pledged fifteen percent of my commission on jobs between December first and the day of the plunge."

My brain quickly went from *Who are you?* to *Oh, that's the Rip I know!* It made me wonder if everything he did had a self-serving reason. I quickly dismissed it, not wanting to keep thinking the worst of people.

Rip put his hand on his door handle. "Careful on the road; it's slippery," he said before exiting the cabin. Yep, that was the Rip I knew; he left me to walk the thousand or so feet to the Alton House. I sighed, grateful he at least got me this far.

Chapter Six

"THIS IS THE YEAR," SADIE EXCLAIMED, sitting in my brother's Jeep. She was dressed in sweatpants and a parka. Wool socks peeked out from beneath the sandals she'd dug out of her closet last night. Hugging a few towels and a blanket, she added, "I'm going to do it. It's going to happen."

Sadie had always wanted to participate in the Polar Plunge but had always chickened out. I sat in the backseat with my camera bag, enjoying the warmth from the rear vents.

"Of course it's gonna happen," my brother replied. "I'm not doing it by myself."

I smiled at the exchange. I could almost picture Alex carrying Sadie back up the frozen sand to the car, soaked yet galant. "Just jump right in," I said. "The faster you go in, the faster it will be over."

Outside the tinted windows, I could see several people doing the same thing as us: sitting in the heat of their cars until it was time to face the Polar Plunge. Of course, the people not participating—coordinators from the hospital, sponsors, supportive family members, and onlookers— were already making their way to the small cove that parents used to entertain their children on the hottest days of summer.

"Okay," Sadie said, once again psyching herself up for this bucket list event. "I'm ready. Let's do this!"

Without waiting for a response, Sadie slipped out of the passenger seat and into the cold morning air. My brother yanked his keys out of the ignition and followed her. I, on the other hand, lingered a few moments, absorbing the last tendrils of warmth. When the thoughts of sun-soaked December mornings in Albuquerque started to push their way to the front of my thoughts, I let the cold air racing across the river slap them away as I jumped out of the Jeep.

I leaned against the grill of the vehicle as I fiddled with the settings on my camera. It was easy to tell who were the Polar Plunge participants and who were the supportive counterparts. Those ready to strip wore layers easy to remove: sweatpants that didn't protect from the wind, flannel-lined sleeping bags wrapped around event-themed t-shirts, and thick socks with sandals. They didn't wear hats, their necks weren't buried in long scarves, nor were their winter boots or snow pants that blocked the chill. Sadie was jumping up and down, hugging herself as she met with some of the nurses from the hospital—all of whom wore matching, hand-painted sweaters that read "Numb Nurses." I snapped a quick picture of their red cheeks, their faces alight with anticipation as the Eighth Annual Polar Plunge banner grumbled against the aggressive breezes.

Scanning the crowd, I was surprised to see Rip among the locals, talking with Willa Corden, the principal of the elementary school, and other teachers. He looked sure and confident, but a chill raced down my parka seeing him in his board shorts and thin black sweater, the hood covering his head. He looked like he fit right into the local scene, rather than stick out like a sore thumb, which was what I was used to.

I moved around the crowd using my camera as a buffer. The river wasn't completely frozen yet. The ice in the middle of the widest part still melted when the sun was high and bright. The layer of ice in the cove had been broken for the event. There were ambulances from the hospital parked near the Alton Oaks' fire truck. As I got closer, snaking around the registration table, I saw Carter among those participating. His department-issued sweats rippled in the breeze as he helped Eli climb the firetruck as my sister watched nervously from below.

The loud screech from a megaphone turned a lot of heads towards the shoreline. My uncle stood below the banner dressed in his stately pea coat, flannel scarf, and leather mittens. The black earmuffs made his hair look silver and it suddenly struck me how much older he looked.

"Good morning!" my uncle greeted, holding the megaphone in one hand and a half sheet of paper in the other. "Thank you for coming out today and participating in Alton Oaks' Eighth Annual Polar Plunge." He paused as the crowd cheered.

"Welcome to the citizens who come out each year, the brave souls who are plunging the first time, and to those who travel to our beautiful town for this event each year. Thanks to your pledges, we've managed to, once again, beat our record for the previous year. Polar Plunge 2016 has raised $10,210 to donate to St. Collette's Children's Hospital!" There was applause with a few hearty shouts and enthusiastic whistles from the crowd.

I positioned myself on the west end of the cove as my uncle talked about safety, frostbite, and proper recovery.

"Not once have we lost a soul—or a toe—to this event; let us not break *that* record!" my uncle joked, inspiring a few light-hearted chuckles. "Okay, plungers," my uncle began as waves of anticipation rolled off the crowd. "This year we have Ches Simons of Boy Scout Troop 280 counting down this year's plunge."

My uncle handed the megaphone to a middle school-aged boy dressed in a scout uniform that barely peeked out from beneath his bright blue jacket. As the youth's cracking voice counted down from ten, the plungers quickly stripped their warmest layer, discarding them to their warmly dressed friends or to a pile on the sand. In their t-shirts and shorts, the participants jumped in excitement until Ches' voice shouted, "Plunge!" and a wave of eager (and some reluctant) people dashed into the water that churned and splashed as people entered.

Excited screams and yells of shock rolled across the cove as many participants ran back to shore for their warm layers. My finger pressed the shutter button unforgivingly, snapping every moment I could to capture the emotions: the gasp from the icy teeth of the wind, or the sharp claws of the ferocious water; the pride that comes from hiding under a dark green, comforter after doing one of the most insane things of your life; the crinkled forehead of regret when you can't feel your toes as you walk across the sand; the relief of support as your friends huddle around you, showering you with layers and their own body heat while patting your back or exchanging high fives.

I caught Sadie prancing back to her pile of blankets, straight-backed and pale-faced. Alex was just behind her, wrapping her in a large beach towel and blanket before taking care of himself. He rubbed her shoulders as she tucked herself into his chest from beneath her cocoon.

The sound of the shutter flying into overtime matched the adrenaline that made my heart race as I watched the faces of everyone on the sand. Within fifteen minutes, every participant had plunged and returned to the shore... all except one.

No one had seen it. Everyone was in survival mode, caring for themselves and their loved ones. When I turned my back to snap a picture of the ice chunks floating in the cove, I saw the body. "Carter!" I shouted as the firefighters who participated were no more than twenty yards from where I stood. He was wrapped in a towel, my sister rubbing his back proudly. "Carter!" I called again, moving towards him.

When he looked up, I pointed out to the water. The wind clawed at the beach as several heads turned to the river. Without hesitating, Carter grabbed two other firefighters by the shoulders, who were likely numb and frozen, and ran back into the water. Their legs splashed through the calm water, sending small patches of ice into a frenzy.

Gasps began a small ripple of murmurs making their way through the crowd, but attention wasn't focused solely on the water until the men pulled the body to shore. Lifeless, its limbs jostled over the frozen sand and it was fully clothed, covered in a winter jacket—clearly not a participant of the Polar Plunge. The paramedics that were already on scene rushed down to the sand with their medical bags, relieving Carter and the frozen men from getting frostbite.

Even if I hadn't been standing ten feet from where they landed on the sand, it was clear how stiff and discolored the body was. The skin was a hue of blue that would haunt my color palette for as long as I lived. No longer would the dentist's office be painted a calming shade, nor the autumn sky be lit with a vibrant, energetic blue. The image of the Whett River in the summer would always remind me of the frozen stony color I saw in her ungloved fingers that curled upwards from where they rested on the sand.

Another dead body in Alton Oaks. The sixth in eight months. Shock shook the people on shore. No longer were the participants radiating jubilant smiles or jumping in triumph to keep warm. A slow frost spread across them, slowing their motions and senses. When the frozen hood of the coat fell off the victim's head, the paramedics assessed the situation, and some onlookers shrieked in surprise.

Frozen ringlets of red hair, some of it matted in frozen crystals, was hard to ignore. It was the red hair that any Alton Oak citizen could pick out of a crowd. We all knew those red, curly locks anywhere. It was Maddie Prince.

Chapter Seven

"I C-C-CAN'T BELIEVE IT-T-T," Sadie said through chattering teeth in front of the dashboard vents of my brother's car. She stealthily peeled off her wet clothes and threw on a baggie pair of sweats before sliding into the passenger seat.

We watched the paramedics, police, and coroner bustling on shore around the body of young Maddie Prince. "What d-d-do you think happ-ppened?" Sadie asked as Alex tucked a flower-themed comforter around her shoulders, her eyes not leaving the beach.

"I don't know," I mused from behind my camera in the backseat. I'd zoomed in on the scene as far as I could. I was able to see the creases in Jake's forehead as he studied the scene. He wore a wool cap that covered his clean-cut brown hair and his cheeks were pink from the scathing wind. "I just saw her last night at the store. I can't believe it's her," I said, moving my camera lens to Chief Gomes whose jacket didn't quite cover his rotund belly.

"You're not taking pictures, are you?" my brother asked. His eyebrow arched above his messy brown hair, from behind his glasses that were still foggy in places.

"No!" I replied aghast. "I'm just..." I trailed off. Spying on Jake? Quenching an unknown thirst for gossip?

"—Being nosy?" my brother offered.

I lowered the camera from my face, knowing he was right. The Alton blood running through my veins made me prone to curiosity and it wasn't always for the best. It had gotten me into some sticky situations in the past and I decided to suppress it.

"Let me s-s-see," Sadie said. Her arm reached for my camera from beneath the comforter. I willingly let her take it and I slumped into the backseat.

As Sadie described the scene on the beach from behind my camera lens, I felt the pocket of my coat vibrate with a text message. A pang of remorse shot through me as I realized I didn't have to worry if it was Jackson again. It was probably my mother, wanting to know what had happened at the Polar Plunge. Undoubtedly, the whole town knew as the parking lot had emptied quickly. I ignored it, knowing Bailey would fill her it. Then it vibrated again. And again.

"Jake is nodding at something the coroner is saying. They're pointing at Maddie. A paramedic is crouched on the ground," Sadie reported, her chattering had dissipated as I dug my phone out of my pocket.

"Oh my god," I exclaimed, shocked.

"What is it?" Both Sadie and Alex turned to look at me; Sadie with a thirsty, questioning gaze and Alex with concern.

"It's Mr. Robinson," I shared, my fingers busy responding to the messages. "The store's open. He wants me to come in immediately."

Sadie's eyebrows knit together in confusion. "Does he not know?" she asked. Maddie was, after all, his granddaughter.

I shrugged, grabbing my camera from Sadie's hands and placing it in my backpack. "I don't know," I shared and picked up my gloves from the seat beside me.

"Do you want a ride?" Alex offered. "We can drop you off."

"No," I said, sliding across the backseat towards the door. "I'll probably get there faster walking." I nodded at the traffic on Main Street that was at a standstill during this frosty Sunday morning.

"Stay warm," I instructed as I climbed out of the back of the Jeep and slung my backpack onto my shoulders.

As I navigated across snowbanks and icy patches of slush, there was no doubt that Mr. Robinson knew about Maddie, but my naive mind had trouble believing he had the store open to make a profit. No, he probably just needed a distraction—and a distraction he would have. Despite (or maybe because of) this morning's events, there was already a line that ended just before the barber shop. I avoided eye contact as I squeezed past the two children hopping up and down the stoop outside the store. Ignoring the CLOSED sign in the door, I pushed my way inside.

As I wiped my boots on the rubber welcome mat, I noticed the handwritten "Closed Today" sign at the bakery counter.

"There you are!" Mr. Robinson snapped, his head peeking out from the back room. He was halfway into his Santa suit; his potbelly was pronounced beneath the red t-shirt and frayed suspenders. "You're cashier today, too," he barked and disappeared into the shadows with grunts and mumbles.

I looked around at the dark store and regretted not bringing a thermos of coffee. If it was just me on the floor, today was going to be painful. I wasn't even sure I knew how to use that ancient cash register.

Trudging to my corner, I hung my coat behind the counter and set-up my camera. After taking a few photos to test the focus and lighting, Mr. Robinson came around the corner with heavy footsteps. "Look at this place. We were supposed to open ten minutes ago!" he complained, reaching for the panel of light switches.

"Mr. Robinson," I began, already feeling my blood pressure rise. "I'm not sure I'm qualified to do anything but be a photographer." Never mind that the agreement I made with Mrs. Robinson only involved me being behind my camera, but I didn't think, due to the circumstances, it was something I should bring up.

"Well, you're going to have to pick up the slack," he said, sitting in his brightly-lit throne of fake presents and holly. "No one expects Santa to charge them and accept payment."

I moved to the register and glanced over the buttons that were labeled in pencil and covered in clear tape. A calculator, a pad of paper, and an old vegetable can with pens, pencils, and highlighters sat beside the register with a printout of the photography package prices. It hit me then that I had to greet customers, take their photographs, print out their packages, check them out—and also deal with regular customers who weren't getting photographs—then repeat. A small anxiety attack threatened to surface.

"How long will I have to run the floor?" I asked, almost insensitively. "Will Mrs. Robinson be back soon?" I turned on the radio beneath the counter so that Christmas music from the local radio station streamed into the empty store.

Mr. Robinson unscrewed the lid of a plastic water

bottle and drank half of it before acknowledging I'd said anything. The crinkling of the plastic grated on my nerves. "You worry about you, girl," he jabbed. "Now open the store. And don't forget the hat."

I bit my tongue and placed the festive red and white stocking cap on my head, grudgingly, but turned towards the door so he wouldn't see my eyes roll. *Be nice*, I told myself; small town manners were everything in Alton Oaks, especially during a time like this for the Robinsons.

Forcing a smile to the mothers and children standing in the cold, I flipped the sign to OPEN and welcomed them inside.

"I can't believe what happened," a mother holding her lavishly dressed child expressed while waiting in line. All morning I'd been hearing the latest gossip about Maddie from the women standing in line. Several had asked me questions as I checked them out, but I had no answers to give them.

"Did they confirm that it *was* Maddie?" the woman beside her asked. Her toddler was dressed in gingerbread-themed pajamas and kept tugging at the fake Christmas tree beside me so that most of the tinsel had fallen to the floor.

"Oh, I don't know. You saw the hair. It must be," the woman replied.

Though I was waving a red-nosed reindeer in front of the camera, desperately trying to capture the attention of the squirmy toddler in Mr. Robinson's arms, I couldn't help but overhear these conversations. "Do you think it was an accident?"

"It has been icy—"

"—but if she was walking along the canal—they keep the path immaculate."

"She could have ventured off the path," the woman said in a hushed tone, implying something sinister.

"Who? Maddie?" the woman with the toddler said and laughed. "I don't think so. My Kimmy—she's a senior now, can you believe it? She says Maddie was in line to be valedictorian. She had so much ahead of her. There's no way."

"In this town, I don't know anymore," the woman sighed as she shushed the baby strapped to her chest.

I walked to the cash register to check out the mother of the squirmiest toddler I'd ever met, before I could hear the rest of the conversation. I didn't need to hear it, though. I'd heard enough gossip about Maddie this morning. Mostly it was about how bright her future was and how wholesome she seemed to be. There were a few outrageous stories about a mishap with a Canary on the canal, or how the very wholesome hometown girl decided to do something uncharacteristic like walk off the path, and it ended up costing her life. No one was asking why she was on the path though, since she lived in Terryville and she only traveled between Oakie Doughkie and the tri-city bus stop.

"Next!" I called, walking from the cash register to my camera, waving to the mother and her two school-aged children in their Sunday best. I took a moment to drain my water bottle. The store had been crowded since I'd flipped the open sign this morning. Not only was it the Sunday before Christmas, after a town event like the Polar Plunge, but everyone was hoping to catch a whisper of gossip from the family.

I'd taken off my sweater and was down to my bottom layer—a thermal long sleeve shirt. The faded black color really made the festive red hat I was forced to wear pop. I scratched my forehead, hating how itchy the hat was. I took it off momentarily to wipe away the beads of sweat. I thought about keeping it off until I saw the scowl on Mr. Robinson's face as I focused on the camera lens. The children were looking up at him, telling him what they wanted for Christmas and I put the hat back on my head with a sigh.

Mid-afternoon, when the bells tolled for the last mass that day at the church, there was a lull in the chaos. Only a few people were milling about the store as I realized there was no one in line to see Santa. Taking advantage, I grabbed my water bottle and sprinted to the backroom, feeling even more parched than I had before.

The kitchen was colder than the sales floor, as if there was a draft or the lack of an efficient heating system. Mrs. Robinson was always baking and this was probably the first time in a long time that the ovens weren't being used. I turned to the immaculate chrome sink that looked like it had never been used, despite the dishes drying on the rack beside it. I shivered as the cool air plucked at the sweat and damp parts of my shirt. I turned on the faucet. It was relaxing to not hear voices and gossip for the moment. The sound of running water eased the tension in my shoulders and I took a deep breath, enjoying this short break.

Letting the water run, I took a long swig of water. When the swinging door opened with such force that it slammed into the wall behind it, I jumped, spilling some of the water on the front of my shirt. Mr. Robinson peeked his head inside, with his sausage-like hand holding the door open. "I'm not paying you to drink water in the back room, girl!" he barked. "Get out here! You're wasting everyone's time."

Without waiting for a response, he left the kitchen and I pushed down the anger that had been brewing all day. If

I hadn't known Mr. Robinson before today, I'd blame his short temper and rudeness on mourning, but I knew better. There were only a few more days until Christmas, and if I kept my mouth shut and ignored his attitude, I might just make it 'til then.

In spite of Mr. Robinsons lashing out, I took a moment or two longer to refill my water bottle and slowly made my way back to the sales floor where a short line had already formed for pictures with Santa Claus. The scowl on Mr. Robinson's face didn't faze me as my stomach rumbled in hunger and I longed for a jolt of caffeine to make it through the next few hours.

Chapter Eight

THE NEXT MORNING I WOKE UP feeling hungover. My feet hurt, my head hurt, my hands were swollen, and my mouth was as dry and scratchy as a bath towel hanging on a clothesline in the summer sun. Mr. Robinson had me stay and close the store. I had to follow the faded, pencil-written directions in chicken-scratch on how to close out the register for the day and then take the money to the drop box at the bank. I was so paranoid carrying close to $3,000 in cash down the streets of Alton Oaks at 9:30 at night, that I almost called Jake to escort me. It occurred to me, as my eyes darted from shadowy alley to burned-out lamppost, that feeling insecurity in Alton Oaks was foreign. Part of me felt as if today's Alton Oaks was a different town, and I longed for a trip *home* where neighbors went to sleep with their doors unlocked and car windows opened.

In the end, though, my stubbornness won out and I walked quickly beneath the bright streetlights of Main Street, my eyes scanning the shadows and my ears reacting like a deer in a coyote-populated watering hole. It hit me that eight months ago, before all these murders, I wouldn't have thought such dark thoughts were possible in my hometown.

I was relieved when I walked into Oakie Doughkie the next morning and smelled banana bread muffins, which meant Mrs. Robinson was back. My shoulders slumped when I realized how selfish I was being; I was happy that she was back at work so soon after her granddaughter's death because it made my life easier. I needed to work on that.

There were small Christmas tree-shaped cakes on display behind the bakery counter with simple gingerbread men cookies and dozens of freshly baked chocolate chip cookies. I wondered if baking was a coping mechanism for Mrs. Robinson, or if she did it out of duty.

As I set up my camera, I'd hoped to see her face appear from behind the curtain, but she kept to the back room. In fact, she kept to the kitchen most of the day. When she did appear behind the bakery counter, her eyes were red and she was constantly rubbing her thumb in the palm of her hand, wringing out the stain of tears that she didn't show.

Again, I worked the register and the camera, but I didn't mind too much since it was a slow day. It was officially the first day of Christmas break for the elementary school and children were sledding down Blackhill, going door-to-door offering to shovel sidewalks for a few bucks, or planning diabolical snowball fights on the playground. The parents who had yet to bring their children for pictures with Santa, would wait another day or two.

Night fell early, as it does in late December. I hadn't noticed the candles at first. Out of the corner of my eye they seemed like Christmas lights twinkling in the window. After some time though, there were too many lights twinkling in the window of the store. I stood up from the folding chair beside my laptop and printer and walked over to the window to see the street covered in people holding candles, all facing the storefront. I stood in awe of the sea of lights. They filled the street, stopping traffic. Bodies in parkas and faces bundled in scarves and warm hats had backed into the police station across the stretch of road and seemed to engross all of Main Street— from the canal to Oak Street. Candles filled the street, lighting the world with hope.

For a moment I forgot where I was—the anxiety and frustration that accompanied this job washed away. Hope and awe crashed over me and pride for my hometown made my heart swell.

Mrs. Robinson emerged from the kitchen with a tray of what smelled like oatmeal raisin cookies laced with cinnamon and ginger. Placing the tray on the counter, she gasped, putting her pale hand to her colorless lips and quickly joined me at the window. The long black skirt she wore fluttered at the feet of her black boots and she took a tissue out of the pocket of her candy-cane and gumdrop-themed apron. Without a word, she stood so close to me that I felt her body heat against my arm. Dabbing the tissue to her eyes, she gazed out the window—past the elaborate gingerbread house display. "Isn't that sweet?" she said more to herself than to me.

There were large pictures of Maddie on the sidewalk, propped in frames and taped to the lamp posts. I realized that it was a candlelight vigil for her. People of all ages— high schoolers, the church woman's group, scout troops, parents with strollers, curious Canaries near their abandoned bicycles—were holding small white taper candles. As new people filtered through the crowd, they were given a candle with a cardboard skirt and a nearby neighbor would lend their flame to the wick. Chills melted my heart when a quiet chorus of "Silent Night" slipped past the store's threshold and brought tears to my eyes. Sometimes the gossipy, small-town-minded people of Alton Oaks got on my nerves, but they never ceased to amaze me when it came to supporting each other.

With a groan, Mr. Robinson's heavy aura bared down on us from behind and it made me very uncomfortable. "This is ridiculous!" he said. "They're blocking the doors to our business! They're loitering! Such a ridiculous show for—"

"Let them," Mrs. Robinson said quietly, without looking at her husband. "They're hurting too." Though her tone was hushed, he stopped his rant and marched back to his corner, mumbling. I turned back to the window as Mr. Robinson let out a grunt as he fell onto the threadbare sofa.

As the quarter hour passed, a gentle snoring emanated from Mr. Robinson's corner and Mrs. Robinson was entranced by the scene outside. Almost tiptoeing about, I put into action the lessons I'd learned about closing the register yesterday and packed up my supplies. Trying not to break the serene spell that Mrs. Robinson was under, I snuck out the back door.

Even from the alley, I could hear the hushed and peaceful tune that the crowd continued to sing and chills tickled my spine. The last, drawn-out line of the song, "Sleep in heavenly peace," touched my heart so that I paused in the alley, under the security light of the art gallery. It was tragic. My mind skimmed across the two whole memories I had of Maddie, but I didn't put too much energy into it. I was still soaked through with my own grief. It was these little unoccupied moments of my day that were the worst; when the pain seeped through the cracks. And, after dealing with proving Sadie's innocence this fall, and mine this past summer, I was done; I wanted to hang up my detective's hat permanently.

As I rounded the corner of Main Street, I noticed that the crowd extended all the way to Maple Lane, just before Town Circle. Every window in the library had a candle lit and my heart swelled. I knew it was my mother's doing. She might be a gossip-hungry citizen, but her heart belonged to this town. Even the Grand Marquee took down the letters advertising this week's movie and lit up the words: Sleep in Heavenly Peace.

The police station, which was directly across the street from the bakery, had officers outside holding candles which lit their faces with a soft glow. My heart ached for Maddie, but surged with pride for this town. Despite the tragedies it had faced during the past eight months, Alton Oaks had a big heart.

"Charli!" I saw Sadie in her ankle-length parka with a few people whose scrubs peeked out from beneath their heavy jackets. I guessed they were from the hospital and paying their respects.

"Hey, Sadie! I thought you were working tonight," I said, leaning over to give her a hug.

"I am," she responded and nodded to the four women around her. "A few of us are on break and decided to come down."

Again, my heart grew. Sadie's job wasn't easy; she had the patience of a saint and was always on her feet. This group of people chose to spend their break driving into town and standing in the cold instead of catching a nap or resting their feet. For the thousandth time, I thought to myself, *How did I stay away from Alton Oaks for so long? How did I not see this kinship before? Why was I always trying to escape this place in my youth?*

Sadie's eyes lit up as she wiggled her eyebrows in my direction. "Heavy high school drama out here," she reported, glancing at the crowd. "Don't let their mournful looks fool you," she said and gestured to the high school students at the front of the crowd. It surprised me that she would speak so bluntly during this ceremony.

"You know high schoolers think they're untouchable," she added as if she was explaining her behavior. "I overheard this one girl who's ticked off at Maddie because she overthrew her as valedictorian. There's a rumor going around that she did it—to get valedictorian in the spring."

I knew Sadie was the volleyball coach at the high school, but the season had been over for weeks. "How are you part of the high school grapevine?" I asked.

She shrugged. "They think they're invisible; not very quiet about airing their grievances," Sadie said and then nudged me with her elbow, jutting her chin at the boy a few yards ahead of us. "That's Maddie's boyfriend, Jason." She used a gloved hand to surreptitiously point at the boy I recognized from the tree lighting ceremony. He was at the front of the line, facing the store. Though I couldn't see his face, his stance was determined, unshakable, as if he was rooted to the spot, and focusing his complete attention on the storefront. It was almost chilling.

"That's the rumor anyway," she explained with a shrug.

"Who's the other guy?" I asked, noticing a boy next to him with rusty brown hair that was long enough to see that the locks curled beneath his hat.

"Best I can tell," she said, leaning closer, "a brother or friend. I'm not sure."

The boy momentarily put a hand on Jason's shoulder, but there was no reaction from Jason who continued to focus his energy onto the storefront. After adjusting his earmuffs, the unknown boy picked up a small cardboard box that sat on the curb beside him. He handed out candles to those who didn't have one with a meek smile of gratitude.

There was another high schooler carrying the same nondescript cardboard box and passing out candles. Her porcelain pale skin, short curly dark hair, topped with a striking red beret made me think of a Disney princess who sang to animals. As the mystery boy and the Disney princess met and exchanged a few words, Sadie gasped, "That's *Wendy!*" Sadie pointed out. "She's probably helping out to crush the rumors."

"Rumors?" I asked, looking down at Sadie in amazement. How did she know *so* much about the local high school drama?

"She's the one who'll now be valedictorian," Sadie said in a hushed tone as we watched the two high schoolers walk in opposite directions.

As the boy got closer to us, we heard someone thank him by name for the candle. "Thomas, thank you," a young woman said, putting a gloved hand on his shoulder with sympathy. "I'm so sorry for your loss. I know the three of you were close." The woman returned her gloved hand to the stroller in front of her which was covered in a pearl white and pale baby blue quilt over a vibrantly colored afghan.

"Thanks, Mrs. Johanson," he said dutifully. The way he moved and spoke so intentionally reminded me of a dutiful boy scout.

"How are you holding up?" she asked, rocking the stroller back and forth, her long gray scarf falling across her shoulder.

"I worry about Jason," he admitted, glancing at the boy still rooted to the front of the crowd. "It has really shaken him up. He's not doing well. He's—it doesn't make sense," Thomas said, shaking his head and glancing down at his feet. "He has so many unanswered questions—we all do. No one loved Maddie more than he did," he admitted, deep emotion painting his face.

"I'd guess that to be true," another parent added bluntly, leaning into the conversation. She was holding a sleeping toddler in a snowsuit. "Have you met her father and her grandfather?" the woman asked with a bitter tone.

Mrs. Johnason's eyes rounded in reaction to the woman's words. "I can attest to her grandfather's irritating personality since I used to work with Mr. Robinson nearly every day, but I wouldn't say it aloud to someone who's mourning like Thomas is."

"Well, it was nice seeing you, Mrs. Johanson," Thomas said, trying to ignore the other woman's comment, but it obviously having an effect on him.

"You take care, Thomas," Mrs. Johanson said, rolling the blanketed stroller back and forth as the child inside began squirming. "I'll bring your mother some lasagna."

"Thank you," Thomas said, clearly wanting to leave the conversation.

Sadie turned to me with lifted eyebrows. I knew she wanted to gossip about it, but one of her hospital companions pointed to her watch and waved Sadie over. I assumed they'd carpooled and their break was over. "I gotta go," she said, giving me a quick hug. "See you later, Charli."

I watched as the crowd seemed to embrace the store in love and support. It truly was touching. The spell seemed to break as soon as the storefront lights turned off and Mr. Robinson seemed to snarl as he looked out the window after dimming the display lights. It was time to go home.

Chapter Nine

AFTER SUCH A LONG AND COLD WALK, the rickety steps of the Alton House seemed comforting. Even though the wooden banisters were weathered and the paint around the windows was peeling, it still felt like the house I returned home to every day after school. The inside, however, took some getting used to. I still blinked a few time in disbelief, seeing the living room—especially in its pristine condition—and not the weatherized plastic canvas that had been tacked to the archway in the front hall. It was like walking into a brand new house.

My great-great-grandfather built this house in 1914 right after establishing the town. Even though generations of my family have occupied it since, it had been needing some serious attention to manage its upkeep. Rip had spent the past two months working on updating the north wing of the house. The living room, library, and study were all newly painted, the oak shelving had been reinforced and refurbished. The fireplace had been restored to its original rustic beauty, the wooden floors had been refinished and polished, gleaming with the reflection of the new furniture—my parents moving the outdated 1960s-era pieces into the shed.

When we were younger, my dad usually put a Christmas tree in the dining room and moved the table against the wall, since the living room was off limits due to its dilapidated state. We must have been squished like sardines, but I don't remember it being bothersome at all. It was enchanting to eat dinner under the glow of the Christmas tree.

When we were older and moved out of the house, my mother put a small plastic Christmas tree on the dining room table as a centerpiece. There were no magical lights or an animated train my brother and father had put together chugging along beneath it. The green, tinsel-like branches reflected the exaggerated sparkle of the suspended ceiling light and a few mini candy canes sat beneath it for Eli. Now, though, I could just imagine a large eight foot Christmas tree, bigger than the ones from my childhood, in front of the window in the living room as we sat on the u-shaped sectional that still smelled like the furniture showroom in Davenport.

I sighed at the image in my mind and the scent of my mom's hot chocolate recipe came rushing towards me. Her recipe was referred to as the Alton Family Secret Recipe as it was passed down from my grandmother. I hadn't been home for Christmas in so long that I'd forgotten about it—not only how rich and decadent it smelled, but that it was always sitting in the crockpot when we came home for Christmas. I forgot how it filled everyone's mugs; that friends and neighbors knew to go straight to the brown crockpot, which was as old as my parent's marriage, and fill a nearby snowman-themed mug. The house smelled of warm milk chocolate until Christmas was over. Comforting goosebumps crossed my shoulders as I discarded my parka and kicked off my heavy-soled winter boots. Even after my mother became vegan and used a combination of nut milks, it still tasted like home... just with a hint of coconut.

With timid excitement, I was drawn to the kitchen knowing I'd soon have a warm mug of my childhood to comfort me. The calendar on the fridge showed that my mother was at a woman's group meeting until nine o'clock (and, most likely, began gossiping until The Buzz closed at ten), while Dad was on inventory this week, working twelve hours every other day. He'd be home sometime before dawn.

I let the warmth from the deep blue ceramic mug steal the chill from my fingertips as I wandered back through the house until I reached the living room. The room seemed to be a new definition of home; it was more an invitation than a place and it begged for someone to come in and stay.

The ninety-degree corner closest to the study was the section of the new couch where I defaulted to every day. It was cozy, close enough to the fireplace, and with a view of the front entryway. I didn't give into the temptation of the tufted fluff of the couch or the gray knitted blanket that hung carelessly over the side (a project of my sister's during the popular yarn club meetings at the library, full of high school friends that were now gossip-hungry mothers).

My grandfather was a contractor and skilled craftsman. He constructed the back porch and reinstalled the front porch steps when he lived here—when my mom was a little girl. The dining room table was an anniversary gift to my grandmother, but grandfather also made the coffee table in front of the fireplace. It sat in the basement for years, never used, but Sadie had helped my mother sand it down and refinish it to put in the living room. It looked as if it had been more expensive than the couch. I wasn't sure if the refurbished fireplace or the coffee table was more eye catching—or if they complimented each other.

Carefully placing the mug on the table, I ran to retrieve my backpack from the front hall. Before sinking into my spot on the couch, I fiddled with the fireplace and lit a fire. I felt a meek smile of comfort expand my lips as I threw the gray blanket over my lap and unzipped my backpack. I pulled out my camera and laptop, placing them carefully on the coffee table, and then pulled out an old leather bound journal I'd started keeping in a Ziploc bag, wrapped in a scarf that Mrs. Kratsky had knitted for me the last time I was home for Christmas. It was my great-great-grandfather's journal that I'd accidentally found behind an old brick in the fireplace two months ago.

I hadn't told anyone of this discovery, though it filled me with excitement. I wanted to discuss it with someone, but there was also something sensational about being the only one in generations to build a bond with Andrew Alton through this journal. I'd eventually donate it to the historical society and clue Sadie in, but for now I enjoyed sitting in the house that he built, in the town he established, and reading his words.

Carefully, I opened the book, its dry cover flaking off in the corners, and turned the browned pages to the first entry. I hadn't made it through all the entries, but once in a while I liked to start from the beginning. The first few entries always made me feel closer to him, as if he was sitting beside me, telling me about the lessons he'd learned in life, in his long, slanted, sweeping writing.

December 8, 1897

I am Andrew Alton the son of the prominent and successful banker, Joseph Alton. The son of Lillian Alton, the fair and beautiful socialite—so I am told, though I had known her for only a few brief seconds before my birth killed her.

And here, in Virginia—so many years later—I am no one.

I am the man in the shadows, longing for a job and trying to keep the dirt of these streets from his clothes and a morsel of food in his stomach.

There are brief moments when I catch myself wondering if I did make the right choice. Did I give up the life of luxury—the life my father had planned, the footsteps I was set to follow—for this? For the dream that has yet to materialize?

And then I remember the life that filled my limbs that day at the bank. The day when some dark-souled man with a revolver tried to rob my father's institution. The day when fire surged through my veins instead of blood and something I could only call instinct took over. They day I stopped fatalities and disaster. They day I found my calling.

I wasn't a hero, no matter what the people of Ste. Genevieve or St. Louis, Missouri, say about that day. I was only Andrew Alton—not the man in my father's shadow, but the man who stood a little taller, walked with an ounce more confidence, because I had found what I was meant to do.

My father, naturally, did not approve when I stood before him in his lavish office the next morning with a dream on the table and passion burning in my cheeks. He gave me two choices that morning and when I chose wrong, he disowned me and robbed me from my inheritance.

It has been eight weeks since that morning. It has taken me that long to begin this account, but I knew I needed to record it. My mother's journal of the year before I was born was the only thing I had to build a relationship with her, besides the limited stories from my childhood nurse who was long since gone.

Her pregnancy was trying most of the time and after one particularly long absence from her entries, she wrote that the more difficult something is, the more it is worth doing; that the outcome would be well worth the struggle. Though I haven't completely understood the full meaning of her words, I must be confident that I am on this road as well: the outcome is well worth this struggle.

One day I will be a U.S. Marshall.

April 16, 1900

My days have been focused on survival, and writing my accounts of an empty stomach or lack of action have not been necessary. Though I was given my own U.S. Marshall badge at the turn of the new year, it is hard to become established.

I have become an apprentice to Hank Phillips, transporting prisoners. The money I earn is barely enough for food, but I have learned a lot from Hank (though my biggest impression thus far has been how foul body odor can be when one forgoes bathing regularly). This career is not the easiest path, but I keep my mother's words close, repeating them to myself at night; sometimes I can see them dancing in my breath, mixing with the cold air. Sometimes I'm not sure if the dance is a seductive taunt or a hypnotic reminder.

A lesser man would have given up and gone back to his featherbed and well-dressed lifestyle that requires no thought but to please his father in exchange for comfort. I will not give up. This is a choice that I have made and I will make the best of my decisions. I will follow through and I am a man who always keeps his promises.

How lucky am I, compared to the other men I pass by each day on the street, to know what my destiny is? To know each waking day that I am fulfilling God's purpose for me in this life? To know that the path I am on is exactly why I was put on this earth? That is a blessing that I am thankful for each day.

September 27, 1902

It has been two long years. I have not forgotten to write; in fact, this journal has sat at the bottom of my knapsack. It has gained weight each day I neglected to record my accounts. But each day was the same. Sure, invaluable knowledge was gained to become a successful Marshall, but there is no news in transporting desperadoes who give in to their fate without much of a fight. The lack of news sat heavy in my soul, much like this neglected journal. Until now.

I had been following Hank to Cincinnati on another assignment. We were boarding the noon train at Charlottesville without much thought. It was another day on a crowded platform with an assignment that was less than thrilling, but provided sustenance nonetheless.

At first I wasn't sure if my eyes were deceiving me. His face had been on wanted posters all along the Mississippi. The bushy brown beard, unnerving hairless scalp and that deep scar along his lip that looked like a permanent trail of drool was unmistakable as I studied him, avoiding eye contact in the shadows of the platform.

My heart raced and a rush of purpose and passion filled my limbs. I broke away from Hank with nothing but confidence; God was leading me down a different road now. Not once did I doubt myself; not once did I think I was mistaken. Instinct had kicked in.

I followed him discreetly as he boarded the train for

Chicago just before it jolted forward on the tracks. Like Wyatt Earp or the cowboy hero on a nickelodeon, I chased the train before it gained too much steam and hopped aboard just in time.

My heart pumped and the sweat of the chase gathered under the handkerchief tied around my neck. I followed Mad John—he had no inkling of who I was even if he did notice me; I was just another passenger. I watched from the corner of my eye as he lingered in the crowded car for a few moments before making his way to the front.

Amazement and—dare I admit it?—admiration broke through my stoic expression as I watched how he scaled the train in the rushing wind, most every passenger oblivious to his actions. I knew what he typically did in these train robberies and I knew I had to jump into action soon. Each time we had entered a new town or relinquished a prisoner, I had studied the wanted posters and read about the crimes of each wanted man.

Mad John would climb into the engineer car and have the train stopped. He'd shoot the engineers so that the train was stranded. Then he'd rob the passengers and, being a former engineer himself, would disconnect the cab and tender from the passenger cars and take off. He'd usually plan it so that he'd stop close to a nearby farm or small town and steal a horse to get away. This way he could work alone and not have to share his bounty with a gang.

He wasn't simple; most notable criminals aren't. They're calculating though, often falling into a predictable pattern.

I let Mad John climb into the tender, knowing I'd have the advantage if he was inside the cab and I was outside the protective steel covering. It was risky, but the greatest moments in our lives start out that way.

From behind the rushing wind of the tender—my feet securely planted on the base connecting the two cars—I watched as he climbed down through the back of the cab and I knew I only had until the train stopped to save the lives of the men.

The cold rushing air erased the sweat beneath my shirt, and confidence filled me with determination. The only sound was the deafening wind rushing past, tangling my hair that I had suddenly realized was in need of a trim. The cold and severe train tracks blurred past my weary-worn boots, screaming my mortality a mere four feet below me. What my father would say if he could see how unkept and daring I looked, fulfilling my destiny!

I could feel the strength of my heart throbbing in my neck as I positioned myself to cautiously peer inside the conductor's car. Though the length of the tender car was several yards, I could see three heads from the window in the back of the cab. There I saw Mad John with a gun to one engineer's head, while the other trembled as he pulled the appropriate levers. Even in the chaos of the rushing wind, I could feel the train slowing down. I knew I had to get closer if I wanted a clear shot—if I had any chance of saving those men.

The soles of my shoes climbed into the dusty coal cart and carefully crawled my way closer, constantly being jostled by the tracks and falling to my knees on the heaps of coal. Hearing nothing but the deafening roar of the wind was not ideal for the situation I was about to put myself in, but I pulled my pistol from beneath my jacket and aimed it at Mad John when I reached the other end of the tender. The men were only a few feet from me now, which could be dangerous if I didn't keep my senses. Barely able to hear my own words, I yelled, "Put down the weapon, Mad John!"

Naturally, that didn't work and I didn't expect it to. When his crooked eyes found me from my perch, he shot three rounds. Two of them bounced off the steel plated barrier and one of them made it out into the screaming wind as I moved out of view. This told me two things: (1) I had about a one in three chance of being hit by his aim, and (2) he only had two shots left.

As I ducked my head below the steel plates of the tender, my eyes swept across the coals that seemed to swallow my legs. I couldn't keep him out of my sight for a second longer—he knew where I was and that meant he had the upper hand, despite my perch being slightly higher than his. The clouds whipped by, reminding me of the cream my father's cook served with breakfast on the Sunday mornings of my childhood.

The image of my mother in the silver frame my father kept beside his bed crossed my mind. It gave me the jolt I needed to lift my head above the tender car. I assumed Mad John had stopped shooting because he either thought the last bullet had struck me, or he knew he was running out of chances before reloading his weapon. I knew he wouldn't hesitate shooting those two engineers at any moment as he knew how to stop the train, but if he did, that left no bullets to defend himself against me.

Unlike other children, I did not spend my childhood shooting turkeys or rabbits for my mother to cook—oh how my father would have disapproved of that! Instead, I'd spent the past two years of my apprenticeship practicing my aim. I shot as often as time allowed. I took a deep breath and my eyes crept higher, ready to fulfill my destiny.

Mad John's arm held one engineer tightly, one beefy limb wrapped around the man's neck as he waved his gun at the other engineer who was easing the brake. Despite the jostling of the quickly decelerating train, I aimed my gun. My aim was better than I expected and it took only one shot to disarm him. Mad John didn't give up easily, though; he was a fighter. Even another shot to the leg didn't stop him for long—just long enough for me to jump into the car and secure his firearm by throwing a handful of coal dust into his face.

With an intensity I've never seen, he lunged at me, his hands squeezing me, tightening in so many places at once. It was almost as if I was drowning in pain, coming up for breath when there was a moment when his skin didn't contact mine. Already I felt my eyes swelling and my lip warm with the coppery taste of blood. Mad John really was mad and I wasn't sure how much more my soft skinny body could handle.

My only thoughts were to keep him away from the guns and to stay on my feet, no matter how many times I was knocked down. When he threw me into the metal door of the furnace and my arm sizzled with the contact, I realized I was looking at this all wrong. My goal shouldn't be my survival—that was the last thing I should be thinking about. My goal should be to contain him, and just like striking a match, my senses were alight with possibilities in those few seconds of epiphany. Then, it was as if someone else was controlling my actions. Without much thought, I grabbed the shovel, still dusty with coal deposits, and swung it without looking... hitting Mad John square in the nose, sending him backwards to the floor.

After two years, I was grateful I carried those restraints with me each day, though I never used them until now. Mad John lay there, unconscious in spatters of my blood, and coal dust-covered footprints of our struggle. With strength I didn't know I had, I dragged him to the iron piping and handcuffed his arms around it. I had rather hoped he would be knocked out for a while. I knew I could do that if I had to as Hank had taught me how to knock a man unconscious by meeting the butt of my gun to a certain area of his head, but I prayed I never had to use that on anyone.

As the shock began to wear off on the engineers, they brought the train back to normal speed, the passengers unaware of what had happened. Both of the men's eyes, shaded in disbelief, kept glancing over their shoulders, making sure that Mad John didn't wake. I caught them looking in awe from the corner of their eyes at the blood gushing out of Mad John's broken nose and the bruises quickly forming on his face. When we approached Brighton, I had a telegram sent informing the US Marshall's office that Mad John would arrive in my custody in Chicago later that day.

I stood stoically and guarded my bounty, pausing only to pat some of the coal from my pants. One of my eyee was nearly swollen shut and blood was clotting on my lips. Lord help me, but pride filled my soul. It was the first day in my entire life that I felt like who I was born to be.

April 2, 1903

Since my capture of Mad John, more success has been forthcoming. To date, I've apprehended twelve felons— most of unimportance according to popular society. They were simple crooks, some with repeated felonies: a man who burnt down his neighbor's farm, and one loud and boisterous female who murdered her husband. She kicked and screamed the whole way to El Paso. Her nails drew blood and left scars down my arms and neck that I'm not sure will ever fully disappear.

I can smell something bigger coming my way. The heavy scent of something almost too big hangs in the air like an upcoming storm. Until it arrives, I've been preparing: I've bought a new gun, better boots, and an extra pair of handcuffs. There is a tidy sum of money in the bank mostly due to Mad John's illustrious capture if I ever decide to retire... but I doubt that will be any time soon. Each day I wake up full of purpose and absolute confidence that this is who I am meant to be and what I am meant to be doing.

December 28, 1904

For six months now I've been following the trail of Thomas Ziegler—Tall T, as he is known. He always seems to slip away just before I get a grasp on him.

I write this entry now beside one taper candle, just after sunset. I just arrived in Mission Hills, California, and am watching the world from behind the closed shutters of a hotel. The past six weeks I've spent lurking in the shadows, watching, observing. Patience isn't a virtue I expected to hold valuable in this line of work, but it pays off so well in the end. Despite my original thoughts about being a US Marshall, it isn't always action and adrenaline—there is so much patience in learning and studying the persons you are tracking.

Tall T will slip up eventually. He has been getting messy. He and his gang massacred eight band wagon attendants, all of whom were heavily armed. From what I can gather, he has been holding out on his gang, killing anyone who questions his decisions or complains about their share. I watched him from my binoculars do this on a dusty, deserted trail outside Houston. There was no thought, no remorse, no emotion. Just the pull of a trigger and a thunderous period that ended the life of his right-hand man. He didn't even look at the man he had traveled with for the past five years. Tall T never took his eyes off the booty they had just acquired. How could a human have no compassion for his peers? Particularly the one who had traveled with him the longest? The man who saved his life in Amarillo when he shot the sheriff before that noble lawman could pull the trigger? Tall T will answer to the fullest extent of our nation's law. With God as my witness, he will pay for his sins in this world and the next.

January 18, 1905

God was guiding me yesterday. Instead of watching the barn on the edge of town from behind my well-used binoculars and hotel shades, I decided to take action. I watched as the four men who were left of Tall T's crew rode out just before dawn. Instead of following their trail, I felt the need to stay. I felt compelled to stay. I was rooted to my spot in that wooden chair, the smell of the hearth's fire in the early morning air extinguishing. My eyes did not leave that barn.

God led me—pulled me towards the barn that early morning in the cold night air. Do you know what I found? Tall T. Alone. Sleeping behind the sacks of potatoes, bits of hay stuck to his nasty, dirty beard. I was so close to him I could see the half-eaten beans crusted to his chin and the blood of one of his murders speckled near his ears. At first I was weary—was it a trap? For what seemed like an eternity, I waited. I watched. I observed.

When Tall T began to rouse, I apprehended him without a fight. He had been drugged! His henchmen had spiked his nightcap, took the booty, and fled! It was the most difficult, and yet the easiest capture to date! All that frustrating determination and patience paid off! The reward money for Tall T is enough for me to retire on, but I cannot leave this way of life behind me just yet. More than ever I feel as though I have a destiny to fulfill and this is the path I must take.

March 27, 1907

The past two years have been dry—void of much business and adventure. I take this to mean that people are changing and doing what's right by the law, but to believe that, I'd be a fool. There will always be people in society who test the boundaries and those who completely ignore the laws of humanity.

It's hard to believe that it has nearly been ten years since I left home and last saw my father. I was in Oklahoma yesterday when I received a telegram from Dr. Graham back in Ste. Genevieve, Missouri. Father had been struck by an illness quickly and suddenly. There was nothing anyone could do for him. Part of me struggles with knowing we will never reconcile, while the other part of me finally feels released, like an autumn leaf no longer caught beneath a wooden chair leg on the porch. Nevertheless, I cannot stop myself from boarding a train bound for St. Louis to see that my father—who refused to call me his son once more, even on his death bed—is laid to rest peacefully beside my mother at Saint Katherine's.

May 21, 1907

As soon as I made the decision to leave my father's offices in St. Louis and my childhood home in Ste. Genevieve—knowing I would probably never return to see the house I grew up in, or to visit the matching granite gravestones bearing my family name on the hill of Saint Katherine's cemetery—my dry spell has ended.

For six weeks I had been taking care of family affairs, though I was no longer in my father's Last Will & Testament. I couldn't help but see that my father's best man, the attorney who kept him out of trouble for over thirty years, took careful consideration in auctioning off my great-grandmother's hope chest that she traveled with from England in 1801, or the armoire my great-grandfather carved as a wedding present for my grandmother. It hurt to see so much of my family's history being sold off rather than handed down to me for future generations.

I bought my mother's silver hairbrush, hand mirror, and butterfly clip before I knew what I was doing. I left the auction before it was over, my chest swollen with grief, before I knew what had happened to the rest of our family's treasures.

Before departing for the train station, I stopped at the institution that was my father's entire life's work, to deposit my mother's items for safe keeping. It wasn't until I was halfway to the hotel, ready to put this town behind me, when I heard the gunshots fired from the direction of the bank.

Still in my mourning attire, I kicked up the dust on the street and sprinted to the bank in shoes that were not made for such activities. Nearly breathless, I tackled the first man who exited the bank, masked in a dirty handkerchief. He struggled enough until I knocked him out with a firm punch. With the fury of grief and anger towards my father, I cuffed him, but couldn't get the other man in time. I watched as he rode away on a stolen horse, not only carrying a bag of money and gold pieces, but a dingy bag of items that meant nothing to him but the money they would bring. He didn't care that the diamond necklace he carried was the only thing Mrs. Kingery had to remember her late sister by, or that the pristine ivory-handled pistol once belonged to Mr. Vicco's great-uncle who built his dream in America. That greedy man who rode away without looking back didn't even know that the silver brush and mirror he carried belonged to his worst nightmare.

I caught Jonny "Joe Jon" Johnson that day, but I vowed then and there I wouldn't rest until I caught his accomplice: D.B. Williams.

Chapter Ten

"HAND ME THAT STRING OF LIGHTS," Dad instructed as I stood at the bottom of the aluminum ladder, watching breath come out in clouds from the cold air. My mittened hands came off the bottom rungs of the ladder my father was standing on and I picked up a neatly organized circle of large bulbed, red and green lights.

"Ready?" I asked, my voice still lost in the clouds my mind had just vacated.

Nodding from beneath his black beanie cap that sported the Blackhawks logo, he stuck out his hand as I tossed the end of the strand up to him.

We'd already spun red ribbon around the posts of the front porch, planted the light-up three foot tall, dust-covered nativity scene figures in a snow bank below the yews, and my mother had placed fake, solar-operated taper candles in every window of the house last night. The last thing on the list needed to decorate the exterior of the house was to put up the lights around the gutters and eaves, which I'd been enlisted to help with before heading to work.

"Got it!" my dad yelled triumphantly, holding the plug in his gloved hand. "Thanks, Charlotte May I," he said, slipping his spectacles back into place.

My eyes followed the trail of footprints in the fresh powder that covered our lawn. The prints followed the roughly shoveled path that I carved, leading to Oak Street. It was easier shoveling through the grass and gravel than it was to precariously keep to the sunken holes my boots had made on previous journeys. As my gaze melted towards to road, I began to wonder how different (or similar) the journey must have been for my great-grandparents when they built this house.

"Hey, Dad?" I asked, my elbows hooked around the ladder, my chin resting on a rung.

"Yeah?" he called down. His voice was distracted and I could tell from his shadow that played near the hemlocks that he was trying to connect the last string of lights to the new string.

"What do you know about the Altons? About my great-grandparents?" I asked, squinting, and looking towards the roof.

"Oh, I don't know much," he admitted, still fiddling with the string. "You'd have to ask your uncle. There used to be a historical society. Mrs. Lupizo ran it. At the very least, I think she's the town historian."

The ladder began to wobble as my father descended it. When he reached the bottom, he rested his elbow on one of the rungs and adjusted his glasses with his free hand. "How are you Charlotte May I?" he asked with concern.

I nodded, not exactly meeting his gaze. "I'm keeping busy, working...."

"Do you like it?" he asked. He so desperately tried to meet my gaze but my eyes went to my sister's farmhouse in the distance, amazed at how much my brother-in-law made it look like a gingerbread house for the holidays.

"Parts of it are nice. Other parts are... well, like any job.

There's the good and the bad," I admitted.

Dad sighed and his breath came billowing out like a dragon. "One day it'll all fall into place, Charlotte May. You'll understand why things happen the way they do. You can't buy a new vase until you've broken the one you have."

"I feel like that broken vase. All those pieces scattered everywhere on the floor."

"You have to sweep up the pieces before you go to the store. It's not a fun task, but it has to be done."

A fierce wind pummeled through the yard and Dad and I both held onto our hats. When it died down, he motioned for me to help him move the ladder closer to the porch stairs. "Look, I know I'm not around a lot—" he started as we carefully moved through the snow.

"Dad, it's fine," I said, cutting him off. I couldn't take the idea he was feeling guilty because of me.

"No, Charli," he said as he slipped the feet of the ladder into a snowbank. My dad carefully lowered the top of the ladder to the roof and returned his gaze to me. "I'm here. For the first time in your life I don't know how I can help. I don't know what I can do."

"Sometimes there's nothing to do but wait," I admitted. "I just have to clean up the broken pieces."

"That's what I mean," he admitted. "I want to grab a broom and help, but I don't know how."

A sigh escaped my chapped lips. I didn't know how he could help either. Honestly, I didn't have the energy to want to think about it. A sentence hung in the air, but neither of us could catch it. Instead of fishing for it, we heard the sound of a snowmobile racing up the road.

Mrs. Kratsky pulled up into our front yard in her tightly secured Eskimo hood that seemed to scrunch up her face. Her cheeks were pink and after she slipped off her goggles, I could see her eyes alight with life. Her appetite for life was inspiring.

"Hey, toots," she said with a smile. "Your mother said you might like a ride to work today."

I nodded, feeling some life return to my limbs with the idea of such an escort. "Yes. That'd be great!" I said, pulling the sleeve of my jacket to see my watch. Noticing how late it was, I said, "Just let me grab my backpack."

"You got it, sweetie!" she said with a wink and pulled a travel mug from inside her jacket, taking a swig.

Chapter Eleven

THE DUSTY AND YELLOWED CLOSED SIGN hung in the window of Oakie Doughkie Bakery and Gift Shop when I walked up the road. Mrs. Kratsky had parked her snowmobile near Town Circle and we parted ways at the library. The yarn club was holding their weekly meeting in the basement. Though Mrs. Kratsky carried a bag with red yarn and knitting needles, I knew she went for the gossip more than the creative outlet.

There was a narrow trail made by several boots in the snow between the bakery and the art gallery next door. The sound of snow melting from the rooftops and dripping into puddles echoed in the small space. When I reached the alley, Mr. and Mrs. Robinson pulled into their lone parking space. The dented truck glinted in the sunlight that the clouds lent to the town that day.

"I don't care what you think," Mr. Robinson's voice boomed though the windows of their vehicle though they weren't open. I could see both of them in dark-hued mourning clothes. "The business is in my name," Mr. Robinson continued. "What I say goes!"

Mrs. Robinson looked mournfully down at her lap. She pulled a handkerchief to her nose as her husband got out and slammed the door. She followed moments later, grief-stricken, and staring at her sensible black shoes.

"Are you sure you want to open the store today?" I asked, taking in the scene.

"Of course I do!" Mr. Robinson bellowed, frustrated, as he fished out the key to open the back door of the store from his pocket. "Business took a dive since Maddie died. You'd think this nosey town would buy something when they come in to gawk at us like zoo animals," Mr. Robinson shot the comment over his shoulder as if it would echo into the populace of town.

"You're here until eight, like your contract says!" he added, opening the door with force and walking inside.

I was about to bark back that I didn't have a contract, but Mrs. Robinson cut in before I could take a breath and collect the words.

"I'm sorry." Mrs. Robinson managed to apologize for her husband's behavior through exhaustion and the bitter taste of heartache. "We're out of sorts. We just got back from finalizing the funeral arrangements in Sandalwood."

"I'm sorry for your loss," I apologized, holding the door open and letting her inside the dark store.

"Thank you, honey," she said hoarsely. She hung her heavy wool coat on the hook nearby and picked up a brightly colored apron. She tied it around her waist as I took off my warm layers. I watched as she walked down the short hallway to the storefront. The dancing candy canes on her apron didn't seem appropriate against her dark sweater.

Mrs. Robinson went about turning on lights, lifting shades, and cashing in the register drawer. "I hate to ask," I began, my voice stabbing violently through the silence around us. I screwed my camera onto its tripod trying not to seem so awkward. "I expect the store will be closed tomorrow for the funeral—"

"—Of course not!" Mr. Robinson grumbled as he lumbered through the displays in his Santa suit that was wrinkled in the back. "We are open—regular scheduled hours."

"But—" I began, confused, and was cut off.

"There's less than a week before Christmas and we have revenue to make up. You'll be here during your regular hours. I'll be here during my regular hours. And Sophia will be here during her regular hours. The world doesn't stop because Maddie died," he said, almost scolding us in the process.

My eyes breezed past Mrs. Robinson who bowed her head from behind the bakery counter. She quickly dismissed herself to the back room. Through a cracked voice that barely made it into the gift shop, she said she'd warm up the ovens to make a batch of cinnamon apple bread. "Maddie's favorite," she added before sniffling and disappearing past the Employees Only door.

Throughout the day, many customers who rummaged through the potential Christmas gifts or received pictures with Santa gave their condolences. When they learned that the store would be open tomorrow, with no change in the hours of operation, they always left surprised, leaving a trail of awkward silence. Mr. Robinson was tired of answering that same question. It put him in an even more irritable and rotten mood. It didn't help that Ruby— Maddie's mother—came to the store in the mid-afternoon looking fragile and void of color.

Five minutes before the store closed, a large man who reminded me of a buffalo entered. "Hello, Nate," Mrs. Robinson said almost coldly from behind the counter. Ruby looked up from the cash register as her husband walked into the store, neglecting to wipe his muddy boots at the door.

Both Mrs. Robinson and her daughter grew more tired as the day wore on. Every other second I heard sniffling as the local radio station played Christmas hits. Both women seemed like prisoners, trapped in the store and it took the holly out of my wreath, so to speak.

I quietly slipped into the backroom after I packed away my supplies. It was emotionally taxing being around the store so long, in spite of the circumstances. Before braving the cold and walking back home, I found that if I filled a thermos—now void of coffee—with hot water, it helped make the long, wind-brushed and snow-covered walk home more manageable.

With my coat, boots, and backpack on, I slipped my thermos under the red nozzle of the water cooler. The hot liquid filled the container and warmed my gloved hands. I couldn't wait to slip the container into my parka and let it warm my core as I escaped this place.

A loud bang caught my attention at the end of the hallway. Ruby had her back against the wall as Nate towered over her. "She's gone because of you. You know it and I know it," Ruby accused him with pain in her voice. She rubbed her shoulder in pain and moved to walk away from her husband.

I watched quietly as Nate grabbed Ruby's wrist with force, making her gasp. "You don't deserve to live while she is dead," he said. Each word was a bullet that punctured even my soul.

"Ah!" I exclaimed as the hot water filled the thermos and spilled onto my hand. My gasp of pain caught both of their attention and Nate let go of Ruby's wrist as I grabbed a paper towel from a nearby table to clean up my spill.

"What are you doing back here?" Nate asked, accusingly.

"Just getting some water before heading out for the night," I said, trying to sound strong while he towered over me. His presence made me uneasy, but I tried not to show it.

"Does Greg pay you to spy?" he asked with sass.

I shrugged, trying to convey passiveness. "Just getting some water," I said and pushed past him. I never wanted to exit any place faster than I did at that moment.

Chapter Twelve

WHEN I EMERGED ONTO MAIN STREET, I immediately put as much distance between the store and myself as my heavy-booted feet could muster. I stopped below the safe, bright lights of the police department and took a sip of the hot water in my thermos to try and erase the chill that clung to my shoulder blades. My eyes tried to avoid the pastel green and pink awning of the bakery across the street, but I couldn't help but study the reflections of the street in its dark windows.

As I screwed the stainless steel cap back onto the thermos, Jake exited the heavy wooden door of the police station, dressed in his uniform and sheep-skin lined deputy's coat. "Oh, hey, Charli," Jake said. His tone was pleasant, but he sounded lost in his thoughts.

"Hey, Jake. How're you doing?" I asked as we began to walk side-by-side down Main Street. Jake and I had formed a bond over the fall. Since that stormy night somewhere on a dark and desolate stretch of US-16 when I thought my life was over, Jake had been that hand that caught me just as I thought I couldn't hold on any longer. Part of me felt bad that I hadn't made more of an effort in our friendship since then, but sometimes walking out the front door was harder than getting out of bed these days.

"Can't complain," he responded, his head bent to block the wind that ripped down the street.

I knew he couldn't share any details about Maddie's death since it was an active investigation, nor did I want to inquire about it. The silence that stretched between us—save for the crunching snow beneath our feet—held sentences neither of us wanted to say.

"Any plans for Christmas?" I asked and adjusted my scarf when the wind found its way to my collarbone.

"Florida," he said unenthusiastically. "To see my parents," he explained, then let out an incredulous chuckle. "It's not very Christmas-y. Sometimes I miss the old fashion Christmases we had as children with the roast duck, snowmen in the front yard, sledding down Blackhill, seeing the carolers out on the road. I miss having an Illinois Christmas."

I knew Jake's parent's preferred the warmth of Florida due to his father's rheumatoid arthritis. "Well, imagine the palm trees and water. You can warm up your bones," I said, thinking about my first Christmas away from home in Costa Rica. Jackson and I had stumbled upon waterfalls and we drove to the coastline on the Gulf of Nicoya and ate our weight in papayas and mangoes. I felt that familiar grasp on my heart that brought tears to the corner of my eyes.

"I guess so," Jake said unconvincingly. He changed the subject quickly. "So I hear there's been a lot of work done to the Alton house. How's it looking?"

A sense of pride straightened my shoulders as I thought about walking through the front door of the house and seeing all the improvements. Rip had done so much work on the house. No longer was there a plastic tarp separating the drafty and leaky living room, library, and den from the front hall. The railing along the staircase didn't wiggle precariously when one used it for balance. The fireplace was restored and working without a problem. "You should come check it out," I urged. "The fireplace works now. There're no drafts. Rip did a fantastic job. My parents even hired him to repair the loft upstairs."

Jake clenched his jaw at the mention of Rip's name. The two of them didn't get along. It was the classic good guy versus bad guy personas clashing. He changed the subject once more. "Your new job all right?" he asked as a snow plow came down Oak Street. The flashing yellow and orange lights illuminated our path for the briefest moment.

"Sure," I answered, not offering any more information. Jake didn't need to know how that shop and the Robinson family felt like a shadow that pressed down upon my already unstable mental health. As we walked along, the houses we passed had the same blue and white sign in their front yards, nearly buried in snow. Each one urged citizens to vote *yes* on Prop 327 during November's voting season. There was a big push for it and a hot topic around town before Maddie's demise.

The mayor—my uncle—wanted to erect a stage on the riverfront to combat the dip in the local economy. Some locals thought it would be tacky and an eyesore. Others thought of the possibilities: local outdoor theatre, summer concerts, a draw for canaries who wanted more entertainment in our town rather than businesses. I decided to take a cue from Jake and changed the subject. "What do you think of Prop 327?" I asked.

His face left the snow-dusted sidewalk and he raised an eyebrow in my direction. Before he could answer, the sound of a motorcycle tore through the silence. Rip pulled up beside the snow bank on the curb. The black bike along with his black attire and jet black hair stood out dramatically against the snow. "Hey, Charli," he greeted, not turning off his motor. "Want a ride?"

Jake sighed heavily at the display.

"I thought you put that thing away for the winter," I said, happily noticing that Jake was still at my side and didn't take off without me.

"Couldn't help it," he said and ruffled his hair. "I had to take a ride. Come on," he urged, gesturing me towards him with a nod of his head and a sly smile. "We can hit the bar outside Sheridan."

"No," I said, noticing Jake was inching his way down the sidewalk. "Maybe some other time," I lied as I caught up with Jake. I'd gone to that bar with Sadie for my twenty-first birthday and I'd never go again. It was the same bar Jackson had been at the night he died.

The chill between my shoulder blades dug into my bones like a knife until I shivered. I cradled the thermos in my gloved hands, thankful for its heat.

"Your loss," Rip said called after me, indifferently, and took off with a deafening roar as we passed the Kratsky's house. Mrs. Kratsky was in her chair beside the window and she turned to peer through the sheer curtains with the noise of the motorcycle. Catching us on the sidewalk below, she waved and then returned to the screen of the television which clearly displayed *The Wheel of Fortune.*

"Do you frequent bars now too?" Jake asked, his voice hard.

"What?" I asked, taken aback. I was lost in my thoughts about Jackson but quickly realized he was referring to Rip's invitation. "Oh, no." I shook my head. I couldn't even remember the last time I was in a bar; probably to pick up Jackson during one of Jesse's drunken visits, but I didn't dare bring it up in our conversation. "Rip just knows how to push my buttons," I shared, stifling a yawn.

"That seems to be his talent," Jake shared, pointedly.

"Are you done for the day?" I asked, knowing the answer but wanting to change the subject.

"Yes." His answer was short and fast, like a dart racing to a bullseye. We crossed a snowbank to walk in the plowed street when the sidewalk ended. "Not much to follow-up on until the coroner's report comes in—hopefully by morning. I figured I'd get some sleep until then," he offered.

The lights on his front porch got brighter as we approached. The large string of green and red bulbs that lined the straight edges and corners of his house illuminated the life-size glowing nativity scene in the front yard. A wave of nostalgia nearly knocked me over and I smiled at the memories of walking past the house, or having snowball fights under the same decorations as children.

"What?" Jake asked, noticing my smile.

"Just remembering how we'd walk home from school this way and your mom would have milk and cookies on the kitchen table when you got home," I shared as a chilling breeze scraped across our faces.

"She only gave me cookies when she knew you were coming over." A smile cracked his face and lines appeared around his eyes. "Four chocolate chip cookies and an Oreo cut in half," he responded.

"We would each take a half of the Oreo and clash them together like we saw people on TV do with their fancy glasses and say 'Cheers!'" I reminisced.

As we approached his front stairs, he said, "I might have some stale cookies in the pantry, if you want to bask in nostalgia."

A smile crossed my lips as I thought about it. "Stale

cookies?" I asked, as if I was weighing it as an option. "You make it sound so appealing, but I think I'll pass," I said as Jake leaned his weight onto the iron banister.

"Your loss," he said with a smirk. "I think I might have a carton of milk that expired last week too."

The smile on my lips grew larger and I rolled my eyes at his sense of humor. "I'll see you later, Jake," I said, shivering in a strong wind; the chill between my shoulder blades sunk its teeth deeper into my bones.

"Goodbye, Charli," Jake called after me.

Inside the Alton house, the smell of a fresh wreath hung in the air. The boy scouts sold them door-to-door each year and today must've been the day they visited this side of town. I also would bet my mother had a scented candle hiding somewhere in the house that added to the festive scent.

I heard the sound of the television drifting down the stairs and guessed that my mother was home and in her bedroom. As a kid, I remembered crawling into bed with her to watch one of her reality shows or a nineties sitcom.

Exhaustion hung around me like a cloud, squeezing the muscles in my legs and shoulders, but failed to slow down my mind. One lamp glowed in the corner of the living room, pulling me in like a moth. I sunk onto the couch, still in my winter jacket, taking a few moments to let my mind settle and to warm up my core before I went to bed.

My mind was restless, though my body was extremely relaxed and comfortable. Almost without thinking about it, my hand slid into my backpack and I pulled out my great-great-grandfather's journal. I ran my hand over the cracked leather humbly. These pages—this old fragile book I kept wrapped in a soft scarf and inside a plastic baggie—was a window to another world. I glimpse into my past. A thread that pulled me towards a past that didn't belong to me, but it belonged to the blood coursing through my body.

The familiar rush of curiosity and excitement flushed through me as I opened the book and fingered through the delicate pages, skimming past his thin, slanted writing that had browned with age.

Chapter Thirteen

April 30, 1909

IT HASN'T BEEN QUITE SIX MONTHS since I've followed D.B. Williams across several states and back again. He is elusive. It's like trying to hold a fish in your hand when it's covered in slime. It's infuriating!

I followed him to Yuma—he held up a bank and left before they even knew the money was missing! That is unbelievable! And I lost him there. I'm not even sure how he got away.

I'm traveling by train now to Tulsa, where he was last seen. I bet every dollar I have that he will not be there once I arrive, but if I trace his footsteps, it will give me the chance to understand him better: to understand his motives, his needs, his thought processes, his patterns. Every day that passes without catching him is another day in learning how to catch him.

August 30, 1909
Ten months!
I thought I had him in Oklahoma City—I would have bet my entire life savings on it!—but he slipped away. Again! How does he keep doing that?

I've heard mumblings of gold being transported in Amarillo and D.B.'s stench is all over that opportunity.

He will be caught and I will be the one to bring him to justice, if it's the last thing I do!

May 15, 1910

It's infuriating when there's something right in front of you, but just out of reach! Eighteen months I've spent chasing D.B. Williams. It is a true game of cat and mouse! Just when I think I have him, he does the opposite of what I expect. Or he slithers away while I apprehend his accomplices. He winked at me as he rode away from Springfield last month. Winked!

He knows who I am. He knows what I want. It is all a game to him and I have become the jester. His pomposity will be his downfall, mark my words. He is over-confident and knows he can do most of the jobs alone but employs men to distract the law from himself. Oh, he is cunning!

That wink haunts me. He knows he has the upper hand. He can anticipate my moves before I can. The fact that an outlaw like him knows me better than I know myself makes me want to catch him even more!

February 28, 1912

I must admit; I've been distracted.

Something happened to me that never has happened before.

I was following D.B. From Chicago, just after Christmas. He was headed west, towards Iowa City, so I boarded a train for Moline. Once on board, my breath was stolen by the most beautiful woman I have ever seen. Her long brown hair was curled delicately and her eyes were as blue as the skies in the south. Through her thick Norwegian accent, we talked and I had momentarily forgotten about D.B. And why I was on this train... other than to meet my destiny.

Without a doubt, she is the woman I will marry. When I am with her, nothing else seems to matter; nothing but her happiness and mine.

June 8, 1913
I have been spending more and more time with Agnes—our wedding is in a few short weeks! She has been ever so patient with me and my unorthodox career. Even that one Sunday she proved she is more than I ever deserve:

We were leaving church that Sunday afternoon in Moline. Stepping out into the bright sunshine, the only thing on my mind was the sermon and the bright smile that crossed my love's lips, as beautiful days often do. There, across the street, not twenty yards away was D.B., staring right at me with his cocky smile—as if he were waiting for me; dangling himself as bait for my attention!

It was the moment the destiny of my career crossed the path of Agnes. My worlds collided and, for a few moments, jostled between citizens in their Sunday best. I stood dumbfounded.

He wanted me to chase him, as if he missed my constant vigilance. And I fell for it. I took chase, leaping off the church's stairs in my best shoes, and didn't stop trailing his tail until we reached Massachusetts when I lost him.

Frustrated at his talent for disappearing with ease, I returned home to Agnes who—Lord bless her kind heart— understood.

She is and forever will be my home.

Chapter Fourteen

MY FATHER'S ADVICE PLAYED on repeat in my head most of my sleepless night. It echoed between my ears as the wind howled and the branches of the trees scraped against the side of the house throughout the night.

As the sun rose over the snow-covered town, I sat on the edge of my twin-sized bed—the quilt crumpled and halfway on the floor—putting on a pair of warm wool socks—and decided to visit my uncle before spending the day at Oakie Doughkie bakery.

As I climbed the stairs of Town Hall, I couldn't remember the last time I was in my uncle's office. It was probably years ago when my aunt was alive and the walls were covered in wood paneling instead of the deep, inviting, fall-sky blue with white accents against the garland of holly and scent of fresh rosemary.

A Christmas tree covered in gold garland and red bows stood near the old fireplace. A sign printed on computer paper was on display at the front desk, informing the staff of a holiday party at three o'clock that day while instrumental holiday music played on a hidden speaker.

The stairs to the second floor had an antique charm

with their nicks and scratches and layers of varnish. I always wondered how many of my ancestors had climbed these stairs. Did Andrew Alton descend from them before his untimely death? Did his son occupy the same office that his great-grandson now worked in?

I didn't have to knock when I reached my uncle's office; the double doors were wide open. Uncle Randy was seated behind his wide desk, facing the door. Large ceiling-to-floor windows made up the wall behind him. The gray river reflected melancholy clouds choking out the sunshine. The opposite wall had a large, hand-drawn map, fluid in water colors that described the town. It was outdated, I noticed. The visitor's center was missing and the gardens weren't as extensive as they are today.

My uncle wore a dark green, collared shirt with a candy-cane striped necktie. When he looked up from his computer screen, I saw a glimpse of my mother's high eyebrows and strong jawline in his features. "Charli!" he greeted enthusiastically, rising from his chair. "How're you doing?" he asked with a hug. I had grown to hate that question. So many people have asked, but I could see the wince hiding behind their brow, hoping I wouldn't choose them to confide in. "I'm here if you need to talk," he said.

Suddenly, I was aware of the pain that had filled him when he'd lost his wife... and that it wasn't the same pain I'd felt when I lost Jackson. My uncle loved my aunt so much. I had so many memories of being at their house after school and he would go straight to my aunt and give her one of those dramatic, dip-her-backwards kisses you see in the old movies. They often held hands while they sat in their respective chairs in the living room as we watched a movie on the television. His pain after her passing was so real—like it radiated from him and everyone could feel it. When he, Jenna, and Jillian moved into the Alton House, I would hear him pacing outside the bedroom that Bailey and I squeezed into, as if he was burning off the pain. His pain was heartbreak while mine was betrayal.

"It was a great tree lighting ceremony," I said, changing the subject—a talent I was beginning to excel in.

He nodded and motioned for me to sit on one of the cushy chairs in front of his desk. He sat on the edge of his desk, holding his hands in his lap. "What can I do for you, Charli?"

I fidgeted with the zipper on my parka. "Dad said I should come talk to you," I shared.

Concerned deepen the lines around his eyes. "What about?"

"I'm looking for some information on our family history."

Uncle Randy looked surprised. "What brings this about?"

I shrugged and thought of Andrew Alton's journal in the bag at my feet. It was a great discovery, but I had the urge to keep it to myself for the time being. My eyes traveled out the window to the birds flying above the river. "Just curious about the Altons," I said passively.

A few moments had passed and my uncle seemed to relax, letting his elbows sink to his hips. "Your aunt," he started—and no matter how much time that passed since she died, his eyebrows still knitted together in pain when he mentioned her. "She used to run this historical society—the Alton Oaks museum. She knew all the stories. I remember her telling you stories about the Altons and about the town when she'd baby sit. She would tell anyone who'd listen."

"There was a museum?" I asked.

My uncle nodded noncommittally as he rose from his

perch on the corner of his desk and walked towards the window. "Technically," he admitted, "it was a corner of the visitor's center. It closed in the early nineties, but everything was boxed and stored in the basement here. I can take you there, if you have time."

A rush of excitement filled my limbs, which scared me. It had been so long—or at least it felt that way—since I'd felt anything but hurt and dull pain. "Oh, that would be wonderful," I admitted, feeling a twinge of guilt and not sure why.

As we walked out of his office door, towards the stairwell, keys jingling as he closed the door behind him, he started, "You know, a memo crossed my desk earlier this month about the historical society—which is really just Mrs. Lupizo." We descended the stairs slowly. My uncle's shoes echoed against the wooden planks.

"What about?" I asked.

"Her husband died right before you came back to town," he admitted. "He left a sum of money to the historical society. She's proposing a then-and-now project on historical landmarks. She's about to post an ad in *The Oak Leaf Press* for a photographer to take on the project. I thought maybe you'd be interested."

The idea lit a sluggish fire that started in the back of my head and began to move downwards. It was a lightning strike of creativity—passion—and I nearly begged my uncle for more information.

Chapter Fifteen

"YOU GOT ACCESS TO THE ALTON OAKS historical museum's collection?" Rip asked, shocked. We sat on the sofa by the crackling fireplace with mugs of steaming hot chocolate in our hands. He was almost finished refurbishing the study and the scent of fresh paint filled the air. "I've been trying to get access for months!" he said, dumbfounded.

"It's just a dusty, locked-up room in the basement of Town Hall. Why are you so interested anyway?"

"I like history," he said dismissively and shrugged. "It's my degree from Columbia. My thesis was on my family's impact on Illinois history," he shared and pulled the blue snowman-themed mug to his lips. The marshmallows bobbed dangerously close to the rim.

I was taken aback at the amount of personal information he offered. It hit me that I really didn't know much about Rip except for the rumors that came to town with him. Was he really from Chicago? Had he spent time in the Cook County Jail? Was he an undercover cop, now retired from all the danger he'd been in? I suddenly felt the urge to share Andrew Alton's journal with him. Maybe I could use his help in researching my family. I leaned over my backpack, just as the front door opened, letting in a wave of cold air.

Sadie's voice found me before she did. "I hope that's the famous Alton hot chocolate I smell," she remarked as I saw her shadow dancing on the wall behind us as she took off her coat in the front hall. I'd forgotten that she and Alex were bringing a Christmas tree over tonight to decorate. I decided it wasn't the best time to pull out the journal.

"In the crockpot on the kitchen table," I called over my shoulder and turned back to Rip. The baseball cap he wore was backwards and the fire danced in his hazel eyes. "The secret ingredient is peppermint schnapps," I shared, "but don't tell Sadie; she thinks it's the magic of candy canes."

Rip's eyebrows twitched in amusement as he drained his mug. He stood and placed it on the new end table my mother had picked up in Davenport last weekend. "I should go. Not much I can do here 'til the paint dries," he said.

"We got the biggest tree we could find," my dad stated as he and Alex awkwardly carried a large fir tree, tethered with rope, through the front door.

"You can stay," I said, sitting in my corner of the couch, not making a move to help my father and brother.

"Nah," Rip said and stood, "looks like a family thing. Besides, I have business in Bloomington."

Dad and Alex placed the tree in the corner of the room, beside the window seat that Rip had rebuilt. An empty tree stand stood there with an embroidered tree skirt my great-great-grandmother had made for her daughter-in-law's first Christmas. The amount of family history around me always surprised me, though I grew up with it; it was something I always took for granted.

I followed Rip to the foyer. As my dad exchanged pleasantries with Rip, my brother grabbed me by throwing his arm around my shoulder. "Take a deep breath, Charli," Alex said, proudly gazing at the bundled tree. I could still feel the chill clinging to his pea coat. "That is a genuine balsam fir tree," he said proudly.

"It smells wonderful," I admitted. A twinge of grief entered my bloodstream like a poison. The last time I'd had a real Christmas tree was during my second year of marriage. Jackson and I went to a tree farm outside Albuquerque and cut down our own three-foot tall tree. It was my last normal Christmas with him; the last Christmas he came to Alton Oaks with me for the holidays; the last time he left Illinois alive.

"Hey, Charli!" Rip called as he put on his coat. "Please let me come with you the next time you visit the historical society?"

I nodded with a smile, even though I didn't plan on going back. I found more information in my great-great-grandfather's journal than in that basement of musty boxes. I already knew my next step was to check periodicals from the early nineteenth century.

As Rip closed the oak storm door behind him—the bells of the wreath signaled his exit—Sadie came through the dining room. Her cream-white knitted fingerless gloves were wrapped around a snowman mug. A few wisps of her auburn hair climbed out of her hat as she said, "Ah, it's officially Christmas!" I couldn't help but break a smile at the scene.

It was my first Christmas in Alton Oaks in two years. I hadn't decorated for the holidays with my family since high school. And back then, our Christmas tree was set up in the dining room, after we pushed the table against the wall. We'd sit cramped in there for Christmas dinner because we couldn't use the living room, due to its former dilapidated state. It was our first proper Christmas in the living room in my lifetime.

Memories of Bailey setting up the nativity scene on the window ledge, decorating sugar cookies with Mom, Alex hanging up stockings on the knobs of the built-in corner cabinets swam around me.

Alex began streaming Christmas music from his cell phone and placed it on a nearby table while he took off his coat. I smiled at how naturally Sadie looked up at him in passing and how Alex's head dipped down to kiss her as he closed the closet door.

"Oh, Alex," my mom said, coming down the stairs in her red and white plaid pajama pants and one of my dad's sweaters. "Why didn't you let me know you were on the way? I would've had the popcorn made already. I've been drying cranberries and oranges for days."

"Sorry, Mom," Alex said as if he was reading a script. He embraced my mother and remarked, "We got caught up in the moment."

"I need to get the shears from the shed," Dad said, admiring the tree. "This one's a beauty."

"I'll get the popcorn made," Mom said. "Charli, will you head upstairs with Sadie and get the box of ornaments for the tree?" she added.

"Where's the box?" I asked.

Mom turned from beneath the archway that led to the dining room and shrugged. "Alex's old room," she said, "or the attic crawl space above the loft."

I couldn't remember the last time I was in either space. Alex's old bedroom was behind mine—it was a large converted closet in the back of the loft. There were missing floorboards due to rot and old age. An old piece of plywood was placed over the hole with an old rug. Alex was adamant that Bailey and I never come into his room for this reason, but now I half-wondered if it was his clever ploy to keep his privacy. When Sadie and I turned the corner to the loft, it was a pleasant surprise to see the old carpet removed from that spot and new wood flooring lining the room. I didn't test the strength of the spot I'd spent so many years avoiding; I stealthily walked past it with Sadie in tow.

The loft was dark, since the sun had set hours ago. Even in the dimness, I could make out the old furniture no one had sat upon in years, and the yellowed shades that covered the dingy windows. I had so many memories of walking through here when I needed help with my homework or when one of my parents asked me to fetch my siblings for dinner. I opened the door and half-expected to see my brother's room arranged neatly with his belongings.

"Have you heard from Jackson's parents?" Sadie asked as I blindly grasped at the darkness for the pull string I knew was around here somewhere.

"No," I said. A heaviness fell onto my shoulders. Jackson's parents had been acting like there was a small town conspiracy regarding Jackson's death. They didn't like how I'd left Albuquerque—left Jackson—so unexpectedly in the spring. Jackson could never do anything wrong in their eyes and their calls and texts made me second guess myself. They had me feeling as though Jackson cheating on me was my fault; that him coming to Alton Oaks was because of my choices; that he died brutally due to his need to support me as a husband.

Sadie, thankfully, talked their brainwashing out of me because after he died, it all felt like my fault. "Do you need anything? A hug? A stiff drink? A hitman?" she asked.

I laughed. I knew she cared and wanted to make sure I was okay, but she also knew I'd tell her I was fine even if I wasn't. "No, I'm good," I said, finding the pull-cord and giving it a tug.

The loft glowed with the cold florescent light illuminating unmarked boxes and old furniture. Darkness seemed to glow from a far corner and heavy curtains covered the weatherproofing plastic that made a gentle sucking sound as the wind howled on the other side of the windows. There was no longer a door on Alex's room and I didn't know why. The empty hinges glared in the dim light like a carnivorous monster and a rogue draft made my shoulders shiver.

"You know," I said, walking towards the bedroom. "You ask me about Jackson a lot, but I've never asked you about Alex." I glanced at Sadie and a smile erupted across her face as she watched her feet avoid the many tripping hazards. "How did it happen?" I asked.

I flipped the switch just inside my brother's old room and the yellow bulb flickered. I was taken aback at how much smaller the room looked than I'd remembered. It didn't seem like Alex's room anymore; he used to have a neatly made bed with a world map and a calendar on the wall. A dresser with a comb and a scale model of a ship that my dad and he had worked on for weeks would sit dustless while a wicker hamper stood guard beside his door. His room was always immaculate, for being a boy. Bailey's, on the other hand, was always a mess. While my room always had dirty clothes on the floor and empty glasses on the desk and dresser, Bailey would have half-eaten bags of potato chips beneath her bed, multiple shoes scattered across a battleground of nail polish bottles, hair accessories, and her collection of beanie babies. And her closet always looked like it had spewed its contents out as if it'd partied too hard the previous night.

Sadie shrugged at my question as my eyes scanned the garbage bags of clothes and boxes that had accumulated since Alex moved out of the house to go to college. "He used to be your elusive big brother who avoided us," she stated, starting to sift through the collection of cardboard before her. "I mean, I never thought of him that way, even after college. He was like a big brother to me too, but..." Sadie trailed off as we slid boxes out of the way to search for the Christmas ornaments.

"But what?" I asked.

She slid a box across the floor then put her hands on her hips, exhaling. She seemed to be debating whether or not to say something. I didn't push her to continue as I moved through a pile of plastic bags, some rudimentary labeled with a permanent marker.

"You know when you eloped with Jackson?" Sadie asked.

"It rings a bell," I remarked sarcastically, though I couldn't ignore the pang in my chest.

"And how Alex didn't speak to you? How rocky it was between the two of you?"

A prickling behind my eyes started and I rubbed the sensation with my palms, despite the dust on my hands. "Yeah," I said and remembered all too well the pain it caused not only me but my family. I still felt the weight of that strain on my heart.

"Well, that's what brought us together," Sadie admitted. "He was worried about you. He's always worried about you. He'd go out of his way to see me at the hospital and ask about you. How you were doing, if you needed anything. You have no idea how much he loves you, Charli," Sadie shared. "We ended up spending more and more time together and after I broke up with James, he was there for me. It was like one day I woke up and my brain realized what my heart was saying all along. Like one day I woke up and I could finally see the world clearly."

I sighed. "Like you'd been looking out a grimy, dirty window, thinking you're getting through life just fine and then one day someone takes a big bottle of cleanser to it and you can't believe all this was here all along?" I asked as memories swam around me like sharks.

Sadie lifted her eyebrows and nodded, meeting my gaze briefly as I squatted beside the last box marked "Xmas." I never felt that way with Jackson, but I felt that way when I came back to Alton Oaks.

"Exactly," Sadie agreed.

I stood up and rubbed my hands on the back of my jeans. Sadie glowed in the dim light with the mention of Alex and it rubbed off on me. "I don't see the ornaments," Sadie said, giving in.

"Me either," I agreed, knowing we'd have to check the attic, which I really hoped we didn't have to.

Sadie pulled the cord and darkness pounced on the room, attacking the jostled boxes and bags, as we walked out to the loft. The music from the floor below sifted through to our ears and Sadie began humming along to Jackson 5's "Santa Claus is Coming to Town."

In the dark corner of the loft, I reached up and pulled the tethered cord and unfolded the ladder that dropped from the ceiling. A cold bucket of air dropped down on us and a deep shiver raced across my shoulders.

Once the ladder was in place, and I was sure it would hold, I retrieved the flashlight that was plugged into a nearby socket. As a child, I'd watch my father go through the same motions as we ventured into the attic to check the buckets that caught the rain from the leaky roof after a storm. Sadie knew the routine too and didn't follow me up the ladder. Instead she waited until I threw the orange extension cord down to her and she plugged it into the outlet I'd taken the flashlight from and the utility bulb hanging from the attic ceiling, exploded with light.

"Since we moved from Jackson to Alex, it begs the question," Sadie said, climbing the ladder and hoisting herself into the small attic space.

"What question?" I asked, eyeing the cobwebs and hoping a rodent didn't scurry across my shoes.

"Rip or Jake?" Sadie said bluntly.

"What?" I asked incredulous, facing her.

"The town talks." She shrugged. "You spend more time with Rip and Jake than anyone—more than you spend with me I sometimes think!"

I rolled my eyes.

"Personally," Sadie began, her eyes scanning the plastic storage containers, "I'd choose Rip. He's got that bad boy thing going on."

I shook my head. Shock hadn't finished registering at the question. "Of course you would," I said, rolling my eyes again.

"So you'd choose Jake?" Sadie asked, whirling around to face me.

"What? No! Why do I have to choose?" I asked, taken aback by her enthusiasm.

"What about that spat you had with him at the police station a few months ago? I heard it was pretty heated!" she said, wiggling her eyebrows.

"How do you know about that? You were still in jail!" I said, still surprised that this was a fact in Sadie's life.

"The town talks," she repeated. "Wish I could've seen it though. Did Gomes really have to hold you back? Did you really threaten him?" Her eyes were hungry for gossip.

Confusion and disbelief soaked my features. I still couldn't believe the distorted gossip this town caused. I shook my head and denied the story. It was true that Jake and I had a rocky patch in the fall, but we were past that. I still wasn't sure what had happened—other than I was being a horrible friend—but we were back to normal. He'd been my best friend growing up—even before I met Sadie—and I was glad to have that stability again. "Just look for the ornaments," I instructed.

The flashlight scanned the corners of the sloping roof that the utility light couldn't reach. Shadows choked the green-and-red plastic tote as I spotted it. "I think I found it," I said, interrupting Sadie as she shared a piece of gossip about one of the nurses at the hospital. I crouched between a cedar hope chest and a full length mirror, lying on its side, half of the drop cloth draped aside, revealing aged black spots. It was snuggly placed beneath the sloping roof, between the exposed studs. As I reached for it, I hit my head on the aged wooden panel that lined the wall before the roof began sloping. It came loose from its rusted nails and I swore, sucking in a breath and holding my forehead as it momentarily throbbed.

"You okay?" Said asked, rushing to my side.

"Yeah," I said, positioning the flashlight between my knees as I tried to push the nail and board back in place. I fiddled with the deteriorated nails for a few moments before getting frustrated and stuck the board precariously back in place.

"You sure?" Sadie asked, peering over my shoulder and blocking out any insight the utility light might have given me.

"Yeah," I said sharply. I pointed the flashlight on the

box we needed. "I found the ornaments," I said, looking up at her from where I squatted on the floor.

"Oh!" Sadie exclaimed with a shriek and jumped backwards. Her sudden movement made me jump and I hit my head again on the aged wooden panel, causing it to fall to the floor with a clatter and I grabbed my head in pain, seeing stars before my eyes.

"Sorry, Charli," Sadie apologized, putting a hand on my shoulder. "I thought I saw a mouse! Something moved! Maybe it was a centipede," she added and looked around paranoid.

I rubbed my head until the pain subsided, sucking in sharp breaths through my teeth.

"Let me see," Sadie said, picking up the flashlight that rolled across the floor when I dropped it. She moved to look at the bump on my head, when her gaze stopped past me and turned inquisitive. "Hey, what's that?" she asked, leaning over me, holding onto my shoulders for balance.

The flashlight shone into the cavity my head made when it knocked the board loose. The light illuminated the nook between the studs in the wall and the roof. When shadows didn't scurry, and I was sure nothing would jump out at me, I tentatively stuck my hand inside. It was unusual, and I couldn't quite place the texture... although a severed hand wrapped in a starched cloth seemed to come to the front of my mind.

"What is it?" Sadie asked as she leaned closer with the flashlight and I extracted my hand from the cavity.

It looked like an old sack that potatoes or grain came in and it was very delicate, easily flaking off in my hands. A lost relic of a simpler time? I was going to shrug it off as forgotten garbage until Sadie and I noticed the same detail. "What does that say? There's something written there," she said, pointing but not touching the material.

We moved out of the shadowed corner and crawled beneath the bright utility light. The faded writing, pot-marked with holes gnawed at by moths, mice, and time, was still clear enough in the dusty attic: Fort Knox, Kentucky, 1914.

"$5,000 gold pieces?" Sadie asked, lightly touching the faded numbers on the bag in disbelief.

My brain was trying to sort through logical explanations from part of a Halloween costume or a practical joke planted by a family member. The bag was empty, but I felt in my bones—in my genes—that this old canvas money bag was one-hundred percent real. But how did it get in the attic? Why was it in our attic? Who did it belong to?

Chapter Sixteen

SADIE HAD A FRESH NEW RUMOR at her fingertips to spread around town about the find in the attic, but I swore her to secrecy. If she told another soul, I'd take out a full-page ad in *The Oak Leaf Press* with an embarrassing picture of her from high school. I didn't have to tell her which one, as she knew I was there for her top three humiliating moments captured on film.

What's perhaps worse, is that I told her about Andrew Alton's journal, too. "But, Charli!" she exclaimed, "You should tell your mom, or your uncle! This is an amazing piece of history!"

"Not yet, Sadie," I said adamantly. I imagined that my eyes hardened with seriousness in the dim attic light. With hitting my head so hard, and the amount of dust we stirred up, I'm sure my eyes resembled more of a sickened child on its deathbed, moist with tears and red with irritation. "I want to do my research first," I said, looking back down at the crumbling bag in my hands. "What if this journal paints something dark; something that would change this town forever?" I asked.

"But what if it sheds light? What if it gives clues as to who murdered your great-great grandfather?" Sadie asked, sitting on a nearby trunk.

"Exactly," I said as if I'd caught her in a mousetrap. "I need time to sort through it, to do some research. It belongs to my family before it belongs to the town."

Sadie sighed. "Until the town hears about it. Then family claim will mean nothing."

"Which is why I need to keep it a secret right now," I said, looking down at Sadie as the utility light illuminated one side of her face and shadows covered the other.

"Oh, okay," Sadie said reluctantly.

"You can't even tell Alex yet," I instructed.

Sadie's eyes widened and, with a groan, she rolled her head backwards in grief. "You have a lot of faith in me, Charli."

"So don't let me down," I pleaded as the wind howled and the chilly draft crept through my sweater.

Needless to say, Sadie was a flight-risk with the sack of secrets I'd bestowed upon her. She began texting me more than usual just to be able to talk about it. The secrets were burning her up inside and she had to find a way to release them. "I can help, too," she said to me one morning over coffee at The Buzz.

"And how's that?" I asked.

"I can be an invaluable tool," she said matter-of-factly as she took the wooden stirrer out of her cup and put on the plastic lid. Reluctantly, I gave in and let her help on the research side. It proved to be one of the best decisions I'd ever made.

The next morning, I passed our brightly lit and festively decorated Christmas tree, my shoulders not feeling as heavy. I was meeting Mrs. Lupizo to discuss the before-and-after historical building photography project before I went to Oakie Doughkie.

The wind was fierce this morning, blowing the fresh blanket of snow off the nearby banks and stabbing any exposed skin. The sun was bright and the sky was blue, which was a good sign. Some of the snow might possibly melt as the day wore on, but the sky remained empty of clouds; it was going to be a cold, slippery night.

urying my face in my scarf, I put my earbuds in before I turned up my hood and began trekking through the well-worn narrow trail of compacted snow my parents made on their daily pilgrimage to town. I'd begun listening to audiobooks and podcasts during these walks. It not only made the trek seem shorter, but it kept my mind off things I didn't want to think about.

I'd almost reached the corner of Oak & Main when someone grabbed my shoulders from behind. "Jake!" I said, surprised, and pulled the earbuds from my ears. My heart beat quickly as I was listening to a dramatic rendition of a horror story, complete with creaking floorboards and invisible but quick, echoing footsteps sound effects.

"Sorry, did I scare you? I was calling your name," he said, his face flushed as if he'd chased me down the street.

"No," I lied and willed my heart to settle. "You didn't scare me at all," I said as I wrapped the cord of my ear buds tightly in a neat bundle and pocketed them. "I was listening to a podcast; I didn't hear you at all."

"Anything good?" he asked, matching my stride.

I shrugged. "Pretty good."

"Guess what?" he asked, changing the subject abruptly. He looked as if he was about to burst with a grand secret.

"What?" I asked, looking at him with intrigue.

"I won the pair of tickets to the Holiday Hop tomorrow night in the raffle!"

"The one from the Tree Lighting ceremony?" I asked,

knowing the answer already. They were the coveted prize all the residents secretly hoped to win.

"Yeah!" He glowed with happiness at this stroke of luck.

"I remember one year when your parents went and Jillian came over to babysit," I shared. "We were in the living room watching some Christmas movie and eating sugar cookies, and your parents came downstairs—"

"—And you said it looked like they walked out of a fairytale book," he finished.

I smiled at the memory. "Yeah, I totally thought your mom had a fairy godmother or a magic wand or something. She looked so beautiful and regal, like a princess."

"Do you want to go?" he blurted out as if the idea had just come to him. "You could bring your camera and get some pictures for *The Oak Leaf Press*."

The idea was intriguing. I'd never gone to the Holiday Hop before—I was never old enough. When I was, I wasn't around, but Sadie went once or twice since she worked for the hospital. It was another fundraiser that was not only successful, but it brought in a lot of revenue for the local economy. Oakie's would be fully booked—and they specially transformed the restaurant for the night, hanging black tapestries over the license plates and memorabilia, while white taper candles sat on red table clothes and fake rose petals peppered the middle of the tables. Eating in would require a reservation made weeks in advance. People from as far away as Morris—even Chicago—would pay an arm-and-a-leg for a ticket to the Holiday Hop, get dolled up, and spend the night in glamour. Meanwhile, the Children's Hospital received a quarter of their monetary donations from this event, and every child who had to spend Christmas in a hospital bed was sure to have a present under the Christmas tree along with special surprises throughout the day.

"Yeah," I said, thinking about the pictures I could snap—fairytale characters arriving in Alton Oaks. "That could be fun."

"Great," he said, almost relieved. I wondered who else he'd asked before he came to me as a last resort. I didn't mind or even take offense. I thought about the F-stops and light filters and if Bailey had a purse that could fit my lenses. "I can pick you up at six o'clock... unless you just want to meet at the hospital?"

"Six is fine," I said as we approached the police station. "I'll see you then."

Chapter Seventeen

THE CLOCK IN THE MIDDLE of downtown struck noon as I emerged from the library with notes and printouts tucked into my bag. Mrs. Lupizo was more than excited to offer the photography project to me. "It would be the highlight of Founder's Day," she exclaimed. A bit of pride filled my heart at the prospect.

The church bells from down the street rang loudly as the lunch crowd bustled along the snow banks. The bells sound different in the winter. In the summer you often forget them as they're masked by the sound of the boats on the river, or the children laughing as their ice cream melts down their wrists. But in the winter, the bells are strong as they vibrate against the fallen snow.

I hurried across the street and high-tailed it to the pink and green awning of the bakery, hoping there wouldn't be too many people waiting in line as I set up my camera and adjusted the lighting.

The Christmas music on the radio seemed louder than I was used to, but I didn't mind that the beat of *Holly Jolly Christmas* seemed to mask the sound of my late-arriving, heavy-soled footsteps. I immediately walked to my photography nook and began peeling off my layers, in-between flipping switches and pushing buttons, relieved no one was waiting behind the red-and-white striped stanchions.

"And where the hell have you been?" Mr. Robinson asked, stomping his way towards me, a wireless landline to his ear. The red Santa suit made his face seem more flushed than usual.

I glanced at my wrist watch as I pulled the camera from my backpack. I wasn't technically late, but since I usually showed up fifteen minutes earlier, I could understand the impression I was making. The rush of excitement and adrenaline I'd gotten from talking to Mrs. Lupizo this morning had fueled an almost indifference to this job.

"Excuse me, Mr. Robinson," I said, turning towards him. He stood only three feet from me. We were nearly eye-to-eye in height, but his width was a bit intimidating. He had hung up the phone and held it clenched in his pudgy hand by his side. A steam engine of unkind words wanted to burst from his mouth, but I beat him to it.

"You pay me as a photographer from noon to eight. I walked through the front door at exactly twelve o'clock. I usually arrive earlier to set the scene—which is not part of the job description I was given, nor do I get paid for those fifteen minutes," I started, as I attached the camera to the tripod. "If you don't like it, you can pay me for the extra time or find someone else, which, by the way, would cost extra since I'm using my own equipment for no additional cost. But if you think someone else would better fit your needs, then by all means," I shared, reaching for my jacket.

It might have been insensitive of me, considering what the family was currently going through, but I was tired of dealing with this employer. I knew their business was suffering and Christmas was only days away, which meant so was the end of my employment.

Mr. Robinson's face grew a deep shade of red and then purple as he used incredible self-restraint to pierce his lips shut. After a few moments of only Bing Crosby's voice on the radio cutting through the silence, Mr. Robinson turned on his heel and mumbled about respect and the lack of it in the younger generation. Triumphant, I turned back to my supplies and continued to set-up, brimming with self-confidence.

Once my computer had booted and I checked the ink levels in the printer, I took a practice photo, checking the lighting, saturation, and f-stops. "Good morning," Mrs. Robinson said, rounding the end of a line of novelty mugs. She wore her gingerbread-themed apron and her right hand nervously gripped her left thumb. Ruby was behind her, red-eyed and mousy haired, and she went straight to the register.

"Morning," I said. It was afternoon now, but I didn't want to be rude. I sat down in my folding chair and checked the test photographs and editing software.

"Can we talk?" Mrs. Robinson asked, nervously rubbing her thumb. A tissue was tucked beneath her sleeve and peeked out.

I nodded, my eyes moving from the computer screen to Mrs. Robinson. Her eyes roamed the shelves and then swept across her long brown skirt and rested momentarily at her slip-resistant shoes. "Seeing as how business is slow and you only have days left of our agreed upon schedule, could you work on commission only, and only from four to eight?"

I was taken aback at the request initially, wondering if it had something to do with my comments to Mr. Robinson. It only took a second for me to realize how much better this schedule would be for me, especially since Mrs. Lupizo had given me the photography project that morning and I was eager to get started on it. "I don't mind," I said truthfully.

"Could you be on-call until four? If someone came for a picture, could I call you?" she asked, hopeful. Her red-rimmed eyes met mine, full of hope.

I suppressed a sigh; that meant I had to hang around downtown from noon to four. That was unaccommodating. I decided I'd make the best of it, since it would only be for two days. "Yes, that's fine," I agreed. "As long as the store is held responsible for my supplies, should anything happen to them. It would be a lot of time and trouble to break down and set-up these things every time you called."

Mrs. Robinson bit her lip and looked nervously at her daughter behind the counter. "Yes," she said with a sigh, "I supposed that would be best."

I knew I should've stayed and gotten the agreement in writing, but I was so thrilled with the thought of freedom, that I grabbed my jacket and went north on Main Street, looking forward to seeing my dad and grabbing lunch at Oakies.

The heavy doors trapped the warm smell of grilled meat and barbecue sauce when I stepped out of the brutal wind gusts. The lunch rush was in full swing; waiters and busboys were gracefully rushing about like a choreographed dance. Black tapestries hung on the west wall, making it seem like it was a portal to outer space, rather than a boundary to the restaurant. A stack of cardboard boxes marked CANDLES stood behind the bakery counter, and I knew my father would be putting in eighteen-hour days until Christmas. It was his idea to transform Oakie's during the Holiday Hop, and it increased their revenue by forty-percent; he overlooked every detail each year.

My eyes scanned the booths of people: senior citizens enjoying their Salisbury steaks, teenagers freshly released from school and beginning their holiday break; groups of moms with their youngest in booster seats or strollers as they relished one last outing with adults before their children were on Christmas break; and a large group of people in business attire—probably in for a conference at the inn. The room was peppered with employees who worked in downtown Alton Oaks: a couple in Prescott Grocers blue polo shirts, a table full of men in black sweaters with the Alton Oaks Fire Department logo on the back, a police officer I knew only by seeing his face behind a desk stood leaning against the pie counter in his uniform. And Sadie and Alex, dressed in their scrubs, sat in a corner booth—the sunlight hitting them just right so that they glowed. They looked so radiant, that I didn't want to interrupt them, but Sadie caught my glance and waved at me, inviting me to come over.

"Charli, what are you doing here?" Sadie asked, embracing me in a hug.

"Thought I'd grab some lunch; I have some time to kill," I explained. "I don't want to interrupt you guys."

Alex wiped his mouth with the napkin on his lap then set it beside his plate. "I have to go anyway," he admitted and slid out of the booth. He grabbed his pea coat from the hook beside the booth and said, "You can keep Sadie company."

I gave my brother a quick hug before he walked towards the door. "I'm so glad you're here," Sadie said as I slid into the seat my brother had just vacated. There were remnants of steak and a baked potato on his plate and my stomach rumbled.

I stole a French fry from Sadie's platter. "Why is that?" I asked.

"I'm about to burst! I nearly told Alex about what we found last night!" she said. I was surprised that she hadn't. Sadie squirmed in her pale blue scrubs, "I called Evie last night," she admitted.

"Evie?" I asked, trying to place the name. "Your old college roommate?"

Sadie nodded. "Don't be mad," she started. "She got her degree in library sciences so I thought she could help. I didn't give her specifics. She works in Virginia now. She said to give her 24 hours and she'd let me know what she finds. Are you mad?"

I poured a gob of ketchup into the corner of Sadie's plate as she looked at me, hungry for a reaction. "No," I admitted, frankly. "When were you going to tell me?"

Sadie shrugged and pushed her plate towards me. "Somewhere between your work schedule and mine. Wait," she said, dawning with realization, "why aren't you at work?"

"Long story," I admitted, rolling my eyes. "Are you going to the Holiday Hop this year?" I asked, changing the subject.

"Yeah," she said as if I asked her if she had breathed any oxygen today. "Wait! Are you?" Excitement coated her words and she leaned forward. "With who? With Rip? Or is it a work thing? Pictures for the newspaper?" Disappointment peppered her tone with the idea I wasn't going for pleasure.

My phone buzzed in my coat pocket and I reached to retrieve it. There was a text message from Mrs. Robinson. "Sorry," I said. "Duty calls."

I grabbed the last three fries off Sadie's plate and shoved them into my mouth as I stood. "Wait! You can't leave! You just got interesting!" Sadie said.

I laughed as I slipped the phone back into my pocket. "Thanks."

"You know what I mean," Sadie said, brushing away the connotations.

As I walked further from her table, I knew I'd only fueled her fire. Her text messages would increase in volume until we chatted again.

Chapter Eighteen

IT WAS THE ELEMENTARY SCHOOL'S LAST DAY before winter break began, and it was an early release day. There was a steady stream of customers in the store until six o'clock. Nate had arrived to give Ruby a break to fix his dinner, which she always brought in Tupperware containers and heated in the microwave in the back room.

I'd just printed the Lorenzo twins' photograph when Bailey, Carter, and Eli walked in, dressed to impress. "Aunt Charli!" Eli yelled, running into my arms. Since my brother-in-law talked Bailey into letting me babysit Eli once or twice, we've had a closer relationship... and I'm sure it had nothing to do with the three bowls of ice cream I let him have after dinner.

"Are you here to get your picture taken with Santa?" I asked as Bailey began taking off layers of warm clothes, keeping an eye on me and her son. I didn't blame her. Growing up, I hurt Bailey on a daily basis—half the time it was out of clumsiness and the other half was because she was my bratty little sister.

"Yeah!" Eli said. "And to give him this," he stated, pulling a blue envelope from beneath his dark green sweater vest.

"What's that?" I asked.

"My Christmas list!"

"A list? For Santa?" I asked dramatically. "Did you put a car and a thousand dollar shopping spree down for your favorite aunt?"

He giggled as if that was the silliest thing he'd ever heard. "No! But Mommy said I should put down 'coming sents' for you. Whatever that means."

I looked over at Bailey questioningly and she turned a faint shade of pink.

After I seated my sister and her family just right around Santa and adjusted the fake presents below the fake Christmas tree, I paused for a moment to see them through the lens of my camera. They looked straight out of a Hallmark Christmas movie: Eli sat on Santa's lap with his blonde hair smartly combed and styled to the side, they all had black pants on—Carter and Eli's were black and pleated while Bailey's skin-tight jeans were covered in knee-high tan boots. She sat beside Santa, and a mistletoe pendant necklace hung dramatically beside her creamy white V-neck sweater; her perfect hair hung in a loose bun as effortless wispy curls fell in just the right places. Carter, in his crisp red button-down, sat on the arm of the chair; one arm wrapped around Bailey. I sighed and adjusted the focus. "Okay, smile," I said, though they didn't need instruction; their perfect white teeth were already radiant under the lights.

After a few pictures, I sat on my folding chair and began editing and cropping the best picture to print. My cell phone buzzed as the printer whirled into action. Mr. Robinson was busy talking to Eli so I stole a moment to read the incoming message from Rip: *I have a hot mocha with your name on it.*

Yes, please! I wrote in reply as the two 5" x 4" pictures

exited the printing dock.

Carter was at the register, making small talk with Nate and paying for the photographs. Bailey wrapped her black, thickly knitted scarf around her neck as she watched Eli tell Santa a story about sledding down Blackhill. Mr. Robinson listened and nodded, but his eyes were glazed over with boredom. I couldn't imagine him as a loving grandfather to Maddie, or to anyone. He seemed like the kind of man who worked hard—however grudgingly—and demanded his family be at his beck-and-call when he returned home, catering to his every whim.

As the 8" x 10" picture exited the printing tray, I heard the bell over the door jingle and my mouth watered thinking of Rip bringing a warm, sweet drink for me.

"Where is he?" a voice bellowed.

I turned to see Jason stumble into the store, distressed. As he came closer into the gift shop, I could see his eyes were rimmed red with pain. He carried a storm cloud above his head that rivaled the grief I felt around Ruby and Mrs. Robinson each day.

Those grief-stricken eyes drew closer to Nate, and then bounced to Mr. Robinson. Both men watched Jason with a look of boredom, unamused at the scene.

"I'll kill you!" he yelled, pointing a finger at Nate, then turned and gave the same pained look to Mr. Robinson. "I'll get to the truth and I'll kill you!" he promised, holding back raw tears, drawing closer to Mr. Robinson. He seemed to bounce back and forth between the two men, unsure who to approach first.

"Everyone will know the truth!" he exclaimed, drawing closer to Mr. Robinson. From three feet beside me, I could almost feel the anguish that radiated from him. "She didn't deserve to die!" he said, his voice cracking with emotion, despite wanting to sound intimidating.

I heard Eli start to whimper as Mr. Robinson's face flushed with words he restrained himself from saying in front of customers. Bailey quickly scooped her son up in her arms, his long limbs wrapped around her as she glided past the festive t-shirts and bookshelf to the bakery.

Carter stood between Jason and Nate, sizing up the situation. He studied the body language of the three men as my gaze bounced between the four of them.

The bell on the door jingled once again, cutting through the thick fog of awkward and anxious silence. A cold draft of air raced past the shelves lined with merchandise and Thom appeared, scanning the room for his friend. I had to give him credit: he was a loyal and dedicated companion to Jason.

"Jason!" he said, approaching his side and tugging his arm. "Calm down. Let's go. It'll be okay," he sounded desperate and my heart cracked at the sight.

"No," Jason said firmly, his eyes darting between Mr. Robinson and Nate, as if daring one of them to say something. "I want a confession. The only two people capable of such a horrible thing are right here and I want to know who did it." Jason's accusing gaze was provoking. "Who took Maddie away? Which one of you did it?"

From the corner of my eye, I noticed Mrs. Robinson and Ruby standing by the 'Employee's Only' door, watching the scene unfold. Mrs. Robinson stood looking deflated, her right hand nervously rubbing her opposite thumb, while Ruby seemed to fight against the tears falling down her cheeks as she wrapped her thin arms around herself.

Carter seemed to break up the awkward stillness in the room as he took a few steps towards Jason. "Son, I think it's best if you leave," he instructed, as soothingly as he could, despite the situation.

"No!" Jason said, sharp and firm. Carter froze beside a pile of ceramic mugs

Taking a step closer to Nate, Jason looked past Carter as if he wasn't there. The young man was so close to my crouched position from the folding chair, that I could see the threat of tears in his eyes. He stood two inches shorter than Nate but spoke with such passion, it made up for the difference. His voice cracked when he spoke and the threat from his initial stance was diminishing.

"You don't wake up in the morning weighed down, like a boulder is crushing your chest? Why aren't your eyes shaded in depression when you see a world without your daughter? I know what you've done to her. You're a monster and I'll make sure everyone knows!" Jason exclaimed.

Mr. Robinson stood from his perch. He looked less threatening than Nate in his wrinkled red suit and Jason turned his attention to him. "If you don't leave this establishment," Mr. Robinson said, undeterred by the show of emotion, "the authorities will be called." He reached into the pocket of his red pants and retrieved a flip phone.

"Come on, Jason," Thomas urged, grabbing his friend's arm. Jason aggressively shook it off.

"I can't go. I can't get over this until I know," he said, determined.

Mr. Robinson's phone beeped as he dialed the numbers for the Alton Oaks Police Department.

Thomas shook his head, knowing he had to help his friend before things got out of hand. "Please, Jason," Thomas pleaded.

Jason only stood firmly planted, his gaze glaring at Nate.

"Please, Jason," Thomas begged again. "It wasn't them.

It wasn't them," he whispered, his head hanging.

Though I watched the scene from the corner of my eye, embarrassed for Jason, my head now whipped towards the boys. What did Thomas mean by that?

"I didn't mean for it to happen," Thomas added, turning to face his friend. "It was me, Jason. It was me."

It was like the simmering pot on the stove suddenly began boiling over when it came to the amount of tension in the room. Mr. Robinson's face grew red as his eyes grew dark and fixated on the boys, phone still in his hand. He was speaking with the police station and momentarily he ceased the conversation, though angry specks of his saliva still fell through the air. I heard the knuckles in Nate's hand crack as he made fists from behind the counter. I could see beads of sweat glisten from Carter's temples as he, undoubtedly, began running through situations in his head on how to handle this single-handedly.

"What do you mean?" Nate said through clenched teeth. His tone made me relieved that he was behind the counter—that there was somewhat of a barrier between him and the boys.

"Don't," Jason said to Thomas. "Don't say that. It doesn't help me. It's a rotten thing to say."

I watched from my folding chair as Thomas' eyes tried to say something as he searched Jason's face. Guilt covered his face like a mask; it was clear how much Jason's pain affected him. "I'm sorry, Jason," he admitted, "but it was me. I did it."

Jason studied his friend's face in disbelief. He staggered as he took a step backwards, as if to take in the whole scene and re-evaluate his best friend.

"It was me. I messed up Wendy's pie in Home Ec to get Maddie out of Alton Oaks. It's what you wanted. I wanted her out, too. I wanted you to myself. It's all I ever wanted.

"That night you couldn't meet her, so I did. She—" Thomas nervously glanced at the two angry men in the store. "She was pregnant."

Chapter Nineteen

A HEAVY WEIGHT FELL UPON THE ROOM; everything seemed hazy and moved more slowly with this news. "She knew her life was over, that she'd never get out of Alton Oaks," Thomas admitted. "Never get away from her family with a baby. So…. I took care of it."

Several moments passed. A Jackson Five Christmas song hung awkwardly in the air as I held my breath, waiting for the storm. "What do you mean, you took care of it?" Jason asked. His body turned toward his friend quickly. Shock and confusion covered his face but his body seemed to tremble.

"I gave her the phone number of the guy in the city who does abortions. The one in Davenport. The one my sister used."

"Pregnant?" Jason asked, still in a state of shock. His eyes were unfocused, drifting past his friend, drifting past this plane of reality. His body went rigid with the realization.

The pain that dipped Jason's eyebrows made my heart break. Being so invested in the emotions between the two boys, I'd forgotten about the other bodies in the store. I had no idea if the story Thomas was telling was true, but when Nate jumped the counter to pummel Thomas, I guessed that much of it was credible.

The next thirty terrifying seconds were enveloped in a cloud of colorful swear words as Nate and Mr. Robinson attacked the two boys while Carter tried to diffuse the situation. I selfishly stood by my photography equipment, hoping it wouldn't get damaged, noting how odd it was to see Santa in a brawl.

Nate threw Jason to the floor at my feet. He knocked me into my makeshift printer stand as he popped back up, and I fell backwards. The crack of plastic mixed with the snap of broken wood as I hit the ground. My shoulder hadn't been the same since I'd been stabbed in the spring and the way I fell sent pain up my back and into my shoulder. My head hit a shelf of holiday plush dolls and a gleeful elf tumbled into my lap; the bell on its cap jingling the whole way.

Luckily, Jake and Chief Gomes entered the store before things got out of hand. The uniformed men went straight into action as Carter helped pull the men apart and acted as human barriers to the boys before things got too out of hand. Thomas' face was quickly bruising and swelling in places, with blood oozing from his lips. Jason's hair was ruffled and sticking up in places as his split lip began to swell.

"What's going on here?" Chief Gomes' voice boomed as he stuck out his rotund stomach towards Mr. Robinson.

"That boy," Nate spat, pointing aggressively towards Thomas, "killed my daughter."

Jake looked at me questioningly for a moment as he extended a hand and helped me from a pile of debris. I gave a little shrug before he returned his attention to the men.

"And that one," Mr. Robinson said, pointing at Jason,

"screwed up her life."

"No more than you did!" Jason spat back defiantly, wiping the trickle of blood from his chin.

Nate moved to attack the boy again and Jake pushed him further towards the counter to put more space between them. "That's it," Chief Gomes said, his patience thinning. "You're all coming to the station."

"Like hell," said Mr. Robinson, waving his arm wildly in defiance. His face was even redder against his white beard. "I have a business to run. You police have taken up more of my time than I care to admit and you're still no closer to finding out who killed my granddaughter. You incompetent bast—"

"—You're done!" Chief Gomes commanded, cutting off the man.

"It's about time," Jason retorted just loud enough so the men could hear.

"Why you little—" Mr. Robinson spat and lunged forward, leaving the rest of his sentence behind the spittle that gathered in the corner of his mouth.

Chief Gomes' large belly pushed Mr. Robinson out of the way. "That's it!" Chief Gomes bellowed. He reached for his handcuffs. "You're both under arrest!"

"What for?" Nate asked aggressively. "This one admits to killing my daughter and this one's a delinquent who got my daughter pregnant and *we're* being arrested? What fine work from the Alton Oaks police department!" he said incredulously as Jake turned the man around, slapping on a pair of handcuffs.

"Where do I begin?" Chief Gomes asked sarcastically as he cuffed Mr. Robinson. "Disorderly conduct, assaulting a police officer, disturbing the peace."

"Assault, battery," Jake added, nodding in my direction.

"Destruction of private property," I said, surveying the

damage to my cracked printer.

"Do you two need handcuffs too?" Chief Gomes asked the two boys with impatience. "Or will you comply?"

Jason shook his head and looked at Thomas. There was an unmistakable wall of mistrust, pain, and confusion between the two. "We'll come quietly," Thomas said humbly.

The men were escorted out of the building; the bell on the door jingling innocently at their exit. Mrs. Robinson and Ruby had grabbed their coats and followed not too far behind. Their movements were full of jerks of impatience, rather than fluid disbelief.

Rip walked in immediately after the men disappeared onto the snow covered street. "What happened?" he asked, holding two paper coffee cups.

Bailey appeared with Eli, asleep on her shoulder. His long limbs hung loosely and his cheeks were pink. "Everything. You missed everything," she said, alight with energy from the drama.

"Bailey Rae," she introduced herself, shaking Rip's free hand with an endorphin-induced smile. "Charli's sister. Nice to finally meet you. Excuse me," she added and then went towards her husband who started picking up the display of postcards and magnets that had been knocked over during the fight.

Rip handed me the cup from his left hand. "Man, why do these things always happen around you?" he asked and took a long swig of his java.

I shrugged and played with the plastic cover on the cup, mourning my brand new printer, but relived that the laptop seemed to be fine.

Bailey was giving Rip the play-by-play while Carter struggled to put on Eli's coat as he still slept in my sister's arm. My sister's voice faded as I lost myself in

reassessing the events that had just played out. Maddie—
the soon-to-be valedictorian—had been pregnant! I could
only imagine how Jason was feeling... assuming he was
the father. And what did Thomas mean when he said he'd
wanted Jason all to himself? And why did he think he
killed Maddie if all he did was give her a phone number?
Was there something else he didn't say?

"I'm going to put Eli in the car," Carter said, cutting
into Bailey's story. Rip listened with a raised eyebrow,
sipping on his mocha as Bailey continued with animated
hand gestures..

I realized that the five of us were the only ones in the
store. I was the most qualified one to run the store and I
was in no frame of mind to do so. "You both better go,
too," I said, gently coaxing Bailey and Rip out the front
door. "What? Why?" Bailey asked as if I was being rude.

Flipping the sign on the door to CLOSED, I opened it
and motioned them to exit. "Because I'm at work and I
need to close the store," I said.

Bailey huffed at my briskness but walked into the
lightly falling snow with Rip at her heels. I could see
Carter in his car across the street, the headlights on and,
I'm sure, the radiator on high.

Locking the door behind them, I locked the cash
register drawer and put the key on the desk in the back
room. Quickly, I packed away my laptop and camera and
exited the back door, locking myself out. I didn't want to
spend one more moment in that store and left it in the
exact condition the boys had put it in.

From there I was at a loss. The store, technically, was
still open for another hour, but no one was there to run it.
I decided to go to the police station and let Mrs. Robinson
know I'd locked up, since no one was there to run the
cash register and there was no Santa—or printer—to take

pictures.

"Oh, thank you, dear," Mrs. Robinson replied, distracted. Her cold hands took mine in gratitude, but her gaze was far away. "I'll let you know about when to come in tomorrow." She then turned to face me, "Our agreement still stands?" she asked.

"Well," I said, my heart breaking at the pain she must be feeling. Ruby sat beside her, wrapped in a brown sweater. The poor woman always looked like she was freezing. "I just need a new printer."

Mrs. Robinson looked dismayed, realizing it had been damaged in the altercation. If we were close to a big city I could run out and get another printer in a brightly lit, always-open store, but that wasn't the case in Alton Oaks.

The woman looked so sad and disappointed at the news, I offered, "Well, we could do online photos only." A bit of color returned to her face and I continued, "I'd have to wave any copyright I have to the photos and send them to customers via email so they can print them themselves."

"Oh, sweetie," Mrs. Robinson replied, her tissue-gripping fist went to her heart. "Would you do that for us?"

I bit my lip. No. I wouldn't do it for them, but I would do it for her. "Of course," I said with a meek smile.

"God bless you, Charli," Mrs. Robinson said as she squeezed my hand. "Go home and get some rest, dear. I'll let you know when to return to the store."

Before turning to exit the police station, I decided to stop by Jake's desk and see if he wanted some Oakies for dinner. I guessed he'd be busy for the next few hours doing paperwork anyway.

He wasn't at his desk—which was no surprise—and I glanced at the conference room door, which was shut. Then I noticed that his monitor was off and his jacket wasn't hanging on the back of his chair. "Excuse me," I asked Charlevoix, a forty-something desk clerk who was walking past. "Where's Vega?"

"Gone home," he said without offering any more information and continued on his way. I thought it was strange that he'd left, especially since the situation from the Oakie Doughkie brawl hadn't been remedied—as evident from the raised voices from behind the conference room door. Then I began to worry about Jake—was he sick? Was he hurt? Was something going on at the station? My worries ate away at my resolve and I decided to stop by his house on my way home.

Chapter Twenty

I COULDN'T HELP BUT STOP AT OAKIE'S for a roast beef sandwich before I made the long trek to the east side of town. I hadn't eaten anything in hours—if you counted the fries from Sadie's plate at lunch. I asked my dad for two orders and thought to drop the extra off at Jake's house as my excuse for dropping by. If he wasn't home, I figured I had lunch for tomorrow already made.

The white pillars around Jake's front porch were covered in red ribbon so that it looked as if his house was supported by large candy canes. A large inflatable sleigh, overflowing with presents, sat in his front yard and the gentle hum of the motor danced across the lawn as I climbed the salted wooden steps. I held onto the frozen iron banister with memories of rainy days playing with G.I. Joes on this porch. Snow drifts bowed to the lone rocking chair and the red and green Christmas lights illuminated the snow in a festive glow. I pulled open the screen door—the springs still making the tired yawning sound it did from my childhood—and I knocked just below the handmade Santa head hanging on the door, the shaggy yarn beard looking a little frozen.

I had to knock again before I saw the light in the

hallway turn on and heard movement behind the door. Jake swung open the door dressed in plaid pajama pants and a long-sleeve t-shirt; it was almost unsettling to see him so... normal. Not seeing him in his uniform or his carefully chosen "street clothes" threw me off.

"Oh, hey, Charli," he said almost exhausted. "Come on in." He held the door open, his black socks stood out against the red and cream rug in the foyer as he stepped aside.

"Oh, Jake, I don't want to bother you if you're going to bed," I said, but stepped inside the house anyway.

Closing the door behind me, Jake answered, "No bother. Come on in," he replied. "Besides, is that roast beef, I smell?"

"Yeah," I admitted. Jake's arms moved to take my coat. I didn't want to argue about the niceties of staying or not staying. I felt a need to stay, so I put the paper brown Oakie's bag on the white wooden bench and quickly unzipped my coat and stuffed my scarf and hat into its sleeves before handing it over to Jake. "I stopped by the police station after I closed up the bakery and gift shop, but you weren't there. I thought you'd be as hungry as I am."

"You thought right," he said with a smile and a hand grazed across his midsection.

Jake began to descend down the short hallway as I slipped off my boots that were slick with melted snow. Following him, he turned the corner into the small dining room where books and papers covered one end of the table. I remembered how his mother used to make us do one-minute multiplication worksheets every day after school in the third grade. I hated that minute. When the little white plastic kitchen timer buzzed, I'd always look up and see my frazzled face in the reflection of the glass in the china cabinet.

"Want something to drink?" he asked, turning on the light in the kitchen just beyond the dining room.

"Milk is good," I replied as I entered the room, stopping at the refrigerator. A neatly organized dry erase calendar was placed at eye level with neatly written appointments and reminders. All around it were colorful polka-dot magnets that covered the fridge. They held receipts, scraps of paper with notes, and photographs. There was a picture of Jake and his parents at his high school graduation, another photograph of Jake and his cousin who lived in Indiana that looked as if it had been taken recently—both had the beginnings of a beard growing on their chins—and another picture of me and him from the first grade Thanksgiving play, where I was dressed as a Native American and he was dressed as a pilgrim.

"I forgot about this," I said, pointing at the twenty-two year old picture. "Didn't Josh Perkins fall off the stage at this or something?"

Jake had pulled two glasses from the cabinet and glanced at the photograph before pulling open the door and grabbing the carton of milk. "If I remember correctly," Jake started as he walked to the counter with the glasses and began pouring the milk, "Josh was the turkey and cried the whole time because he thought he was going to be cooked and sliced for the feast."

"Oh yeah," I mused. "He had that teddy bear he carried with him all the time."

"And his turkey costume was so big, he couldn't wear it without it falling around his knees."

I smiled at the memory. "And—oh, what was her name?—she spent the entire play picking up the teddy bear and giving it back to Josh."

"Melanie," Jake said and put the milk back in the fridge. "She and Josh were married right out of high school."

"Really?" I asked. I had no memories of either one after the fourth grade.

"Yeah. They divorced a few months later. I don't really know the details." Jake put the two glasses on the island. "Do you mind if we eat in here? The dining room's a mess."

"Sure." I shrugged and sat on the stool on the opposite end of the island. Jake pulled two plates from a nearby cabinet and sat at the stool beside me as I pulled out the wax paper-covered sandwiches.

"What's going on in the dining room?" I asked and remembered the mess of papers and books on the table.

Jake had hungrily unwrapped the sandwich and taken a large bite while I was still pulling out the fries and onion rings from the bag. "Just studying," he said in between bites.

I got up from my seat and found a knife in the silverware drawer. "Studying for what?" I asked as I carefully cut my sandwich in half.

"You still do that?" Jake said after swallowing and gestured to my cut up sandwich.

I looked down at my plate and shrugged as gravy oozed over the melted cheese that escaped the bread. I nodded; I didn't think it was weird that every sandwich had to be cut in half. To me it was practical; easier. As a child, though, I guess it was a big deal. Any peanut butter and jelly sandwich was a disgusting blob that I wouldn't touch until it was neatly cut in half.

"What are you studying for?" I asked again before I picked up half of the sandwich and let my teeth sink into it.

"The detective's exam," Jake said and stuffed a few fries into his mouth. "I'm looking to become a police detective, especially in light of recent circumstances."

I let that news sink in as I finished half of my sandwich. "Alton Oaks has changed," I admitted after washing down half of my milk.

Surprisingly, Jake had already finished his sandwich and was happily making his way through the container of onion rings. "It hasn't changed," he admitted, frowning. He pulled an Oakie's napkin from the discarded bag and wiped his mouth. "It's just that things that were kept in secret are no longer secret."

I let his words swim through my head as I stole an onion ring from his reach. Jake and I had the same childhood; we learned at the same school, played at the same park, hung out with the same kids, and went to the same doctor, grocery store, and restaurants in our small town. As adults, I'd left our town, remembering it the same way an innocent child would. On the other hand, Jake stayed as an adult—moreover, a policeman—and got to see things that we as children never would have known were there. While I was living in a fantasy world thinking of Alton Oaks as a quaint storybook town, Jake was living in a gothic reality where he has to know what's going on in the shadows, behind the dark and heavy curtains that we didn't see as children.

"If you ever want to talk about it..." I trailed off, not wanting to offer something useless. "I mean, I know there's things you can't talk about, but I can keep your confidence."

Jake crumpled his wax paper, tucked it inside the empty cardboard onion ring container, and tossed it into the garbage can against the wall. He offered a small nod and wiped the counter of crumbs with his hands.

"What about you?" Jake asked, turning to face me. "How are you doing after," he paused to search for the right way to say it, "everything?"

I knew he was referring to Jackson's passing and the drama that came with it. My shoulders tensed up just thinking about the lawyers and the phone calls from his parents. "Do you ever want to talk about it?" Jake asked, resting his elbow on the granite counter.

"Not really," I admitted. "Sometimes," I quickly added, surprised that the word even popped out of my mouth.

Jake must've registered the surprise on my face. He responded, "I can keep your confidence too."

A small smile of understanding crossed my lips as I looked down at what was left of my sandwich. "I'm not hungry anymore," I admitted and began wrapping the sandwich back in its wax paper.

"Hey, remember that TV show we used to watch as kids? The one with the dog?" Jake asked, bringing a lighter tone to his voice as he grabbed the plates and put them in the sink. I followed suit with the empty glasses.

"And that crazy neighbor lady?" I asked.

Jake nodded. "My mom sent me the first season as a Christmas present. Do you have time? We can watch the first episode."

"Oh, that would be awesome," I said genuinely. "When are you leaving for Florida? To be with them for Christmas?"

Jake shut the light off in the kitchen and I followed him to the living room, plopping down on the chaise lounge end of the black couch. "Change of plans," Jake admitted as he picked up three different remotes and pointed each to the television. "They're taking a cruise to the Dominican Republic."

"For Christmas?!" I asked shocked that they'd choose

a subtropical climate over the festively cold midwest.

Jake shrugged as the living room lit up from the glow of the television. He grabbed a DVD from the built-in bookshelves on either side of the television and put it in the DVD player. "They're planning on coming in this spring. Besides, someone has to be on duty at the station on Christmas."

The thought of not spending Christmas with family should be something I was used to, as I kept myself from Alton Oaks and my family for more than one Christmas while I was married to Jackson, but now the idea seemed depressing. Knowing that Jake wouldn't be with his family and would spend Christmas alone in the police department made my heart ache.

"Ah, here we go!" Jake said excitedly as the familiar theme music began to play. He fell onto the couch beside me. Nostalgia filled the air between us as we followed the dog on his adventure in the first episode. With it, I think we both began to forget the current state of affairs in Alton Oaks, if only for thirty minutes at a time.

Chapter Twenty-One

THE NEXT MORNING WAS DARK AND GRAY. It was much harder to pull myself out of bed. My nose was cold, but my blankets were so warm. I could've laid there for three more hours, despite it already being ten in the morning. After my arm braved the temperature outside the blankets, I found a text from Mrs. Robinson. Nearly two hours later, I braved the windless chill in the air and walked into Oakie Doughkie bakery, not sure what to expect.

The front door was open, though the CLOSED sign still hung in the window. The festive display lights were off and the darkness of the store added to the dark skies outside. "Hello?" I called, noticing that no one was behind the bakery counter and no Christmas music filled the corners.

Carefully, I put my backpack down behind the counter and walked through the shadows and the 'Employees Only' door. Voices skipped down the hallway from the kitchen. Ruby and Mrs. Robinson sat at the long metal table in the kitchen. It felt as though the oven had been on—the room was warmer than the others—but now it was dark and silent.

"Good morning, Charli," Mrs. Robinson greeted in a

defeated tone. Her hand hugged a large mug.

Ruby was at the counter in the corner, her purse resting beside her as she poured herself a cup of hot water from a red kettle. She nodded silently in acknowledgement.

"Good morning," I greeted, feigning a small town pleasantness. "When I got your text, I thought the store would be open today," I said, sitting beside Mrs. Robinson.

"Oh, yes," she said as if she just remembered why I was there. "It will be. We're just..." she paused for a moment and glanced at Ruby who was stirring sugar into her mug at the counter. "Taking our time this morning," she finished.

I nodded, understanding.

Ruby turned from her spot at the counter and limped to the seat beside her mother and across from me. "Are you okay?" I asked, concerned about her hobbling.

"Oh, yes," she said, making brief eye contact. In that second I could see the pain that rimmed her eyes and it tugged at my heart. "Slipped on the ice."

"She fell on a patch of ice about two weeks ago. Pretty bad. Had to see the doctor," Mrs. Robinson explained. "She slipped again last night as we were leaving the police station. Nothing too bad, just aggravated."

I nodded. Both women were quiet, but comfortable just sitting in silent company, though every few seconds was interrupted with a sniffle. "Do you mind if I..." I asked, nodding to the tea kettle. I wasn't a big tea person, but if coffee wasn't available, it would have to do.

Mrs. Robinson nodded even though I wasn't sure she registered my question.

My absence from the table shifted some kind of emotional balance. As soon as my back was turned, both women began to cry. Abandoning my quest for tea, I reached for the box of tissues that sat beside Ruby's purse (or maybe it had been in the purse and tumbled out, I wasn't sure). A prescription bottle of Tramadol rolled out and I quickly tossed it back into the bag as I put the tissues on the table between the two women. I remembered how strong Tramadol was when I was in the hospital in the spring, and I could only imagine how painful Ruby's ankle felt.

"Hello?" a voice called down the hallway as the bell on the front door jingled. I knew it was Jake before he rounded the corner into the kitchen. "Morning," he nodded. Another officer was with him. "I have a search warrant," Jake began. "Hope we don't inconvenience you."

Mrs. Robinson waved her hand in response as she dabbed her eyes with tissue.

"I don't think you should open the store today," I said.

"Nonsense!" Mrs. Robinson said. "Tomorrow's Christmas Eve."

"I think the town will understand." I encouraged.

"Poppycock!" Mrs. Robinson remarked, waving her hand. "We just need a few more minutes to collect ourselves. You go set up your scene. We'll open the doors in ten minutes."

"But we have no Santa," I said, wondering what I'd do in his absence.

"We'll offer holiday photos at a discount," Mrs. Robinson said quickly, as if opening the store today was a matter of life-and-death. "We'll open in ten minutes," she said again.

I didn't want to argue with her; it was her store.

When I got to my corner, I saw a new TV tray next to the folding chair. Jake was behind the register, going through a folder of receipts.

"What exactly are you looking for?" I asked as I pulled

the laptop and camera case from my bag.

"Anything that might tie in the Robinsons to Maddie's murder," Jake said, without looking up from the folder.

"What do you think you're going to find? A note that explains how she ended up in the river?" I asked sarcastically as I pulled out my camera and screwed it onto the tripod.

Jake didn't answer, but closed the folder and opened a drawer. In a lower voice, so the officer behind the bakery counter couldn't hear, Jake said, "The toxicology report came back. Maddie was on enough medication, you'd think she was in a psych ward."

"Medication?" I asked, flipping the switch on the lighting equipment. "That would explain her excessive studying."

Jake shook his head. "I know some kids take caffeine pills or speed to stay up and study, but the drugs in Maddie's system were all downers."

I slowly turned towards Jake, sober with a realization. "Like Tramadol?" I whispered, remembering the orange pill bottle that rolled out of Ruby's purse only minutes ago.

Chapter Twenty-Two

"YES," JAKE REPLIED, LOOKING UP from the drawer at me suspiciously. "Why would you mention that one specifically?"

I hesitated, knowing Jake would think I was being nosey. "I knocked a bottle out of Ruby's purse when I reached for the tissue box," I admitted.

Jake looked towards the 'Employees Only' door and took a deep breath, like he was preparing for battle. Without saying a word to me, he approached the other office behind the bakery counter and they both disappeared behind the door.

The door seemed to throb as I stood there, waiting in anticipation. Did I just unintentionally solve the murder or did I just scar Ruby while she was mourning her only child's death? I couldn't imagine she could murder her daughter, but she was so quiet and reserved; I didn't really know her at all.

An elderly couple knocked on the front door with their gloved hands and pointed to their watch. My head shot in their direction and I shrugged exaggeratedly to answer their implied question. The Oakie Doughkie Bakery & Gift Shop should've been opened by now, and the fact that it wasn't was starting to draw attention.

The elderly couple began talking with a woman who had two young children with her. They pointed at the store and to their wristwatch, shrugging. Families who were doing their last minute Christmas shopping or hoping to take Christmas photos were stopping to ask why the lights of the bakery weren't illuminated on this gloomy day, I could imagine.

When the 'Employees Only' door swung open, I nearly jumped. Jake led the way, followed by Ruby and the accompanying officer. Without a word, they exited the store and I watched as they made their way across the street to the police station. The people standing on the sidewalk watched unabashedly. After the door to the police station shut behind Ruby, a flurry of energy seemed to ripple across Main Street as people turned to the closest citizen to gossip.

Realizing that Mrs. Robinson was still in the backroom, and her husband, daughter, and granddaughter were gone, I let my feet carry myself behind the 'Employees Only' door once more.

The kitchen door was open, as usual, but I still knocked softly as Mrs. Robinson sat in the same chair, her hand wrapped around her mug, and she stared into the metallic table. Her white hair wasn't as tightly pulled back into a hair clip like it normally was, and wisps of hair were coming loose by her ears. She looked fragile and about to break down at any moment.

"Is there anything I can do?" I asked.

Mrs. Robinson didn't acknowledge me at all, but I sat down beside her, listening to her sniffles. Occasionally, she'd reach for a new tissue. It wasn't long before I got up and helped myself to a cup of tea, as I intended to do earlier. I always thought tea tasted like hot water but smelled nice; I didn't see the point of it. However, the blend that Mrs. Robinson had put together not only smelled divinely of cinnamon and oranges, but it seemed to relax me within moments. My world became a bit softer.

"Is there anything I can do for you, Mrs. Robinson?" I asked again, taking another gulp of tea. "Tomorrow's Christmas Eve," I said, trying to get some sort of reaction from her.

She sniffled and brought a tissue to her nose and I feared another wave of grief would seize her senses. "It wasn't always like this," she said quietly, in a broken and raspy voice.

"What do you mean?" I asked, draining the mug and feeling like a nap was in my immediate future.

Mrs. Robinson sniffled again. "I know how it looks to other people," she began without looking up from the spot she stared at. "My husband wasn't always rough around the edges. He cared greatly for me and his daughter." She paused and took a sip of her tea. "Too greatly," she added.

She sighed and I didn't want to move or make a sound, in fear that she'd return to an almost comatose state. "I was his whole world and we were the happiest people in the entire world when we got married. Greg spent a lifetime of smiles during those few years it was just us.

"Then Ruby was born—my darling, beautiful, perfect little girl. The older she got, the more attention Greg took from me and put on her. He made sure she had the ballet classes she wanted and took her shopping for new clothes once a month. Ruby was his world."

She smiled nostalgically for a moment, then her face hardened. "In high school she started dating Nate, the star of the football team. That's when Greg changed. He grew angry and watchful and paranoid. I guess he had a right to feel that way since Ruby got pregnant when she was sixteen."

My brain seemed sluggish, but I could recall a rumor about this somewhere in the back of my brain. Nevertheless, I said, "I had no idea."

Mrs. Robinson didn't seem to hear me. Her hazy eyes were fixed on the oven on the other side of the room. "I had to break the news to Greg and the only way I knew how was to give him an extra dose or two of his Vicodin one night in his after-dinner coffee."

I waited as Mrs. Robinson's shoulders slumped and she seemed to struggle with another wave of grief. "He said something to me that night that I never told another soul. He was so high that after I told him our Ruby was pregnant he said, 'I know.' When I asked him how he knew and why he wasn't more angry about it, he said, 'The baby is mine.'"

Chapter Twenty-Three

THE SHOCK OF SUCH NEWS brought me out of my stupor for a few moments. I couldn't respond with anything more than an unhinged jaw. "Of course," Mrs. Robinson continued, "I didn't believe it at all. I had no reason to believe it, no evidence, no notion. I thought he was just being possessive. I never believed it... not until Maddie came to me last week."

Mrs. Robinson dipped her head in an exaggerated way, then reached for another tissue. A stream of tears silently poured from her eyes. Demons were tearing up a battlefield inside of her. "Maddie came to me here in the store, crying her eyes out, after the tree lighting ceremony. I gave her some hot chocolate with a little something extra in it to relax her. She was so hysterical and I couldn't understand why.

"We were in the loft upstairs," she shared, gesturing her head towards the ceiling. "We'd just had a tenant move out last month. That man was always having it out with Greg." She shook her head and took a deep gulp of her tea which had to be ice cold by now.

"Maddie, my dear little Maddie," she said, letting more tears fall. "Maddie finally calmed down to tell me she was pregnant. I knew she was destined for college—it's what everyone in this town talks about, everything Maddie talked about. But the news that she was expecting made my heart swell! I always knew Maddie was more suited to be a mother than a scholar. It's where her sweet heart belonged, though she would never admit it.

"I told her that Jason would be an amazing father as I rubbed her back encouragingly. It sent her off into another fit of tears. I kept asking what was wrong—I had no idea! I was so confused about her anguish. A baby wasn't the end of the world—I wanted her to see it was the beginning."

Mrs. Robinson shook her head, closed her eyes tightly and began rubbing her thumb nervously. It was almost as if she was in a trance and she had no notion I was there at all. "That's when she told me it wasn't Jason's baby," she admitted, not opening her eyes. She said that they never slept together and then she cried with so much pain, that my heart clear broke in two. She tried to say more. She kept trying to explain, but she couldn't. She looked so ashamed.

"I knew I was missing some part of the puzzle. The way she felt didn't make sense to me." Mrs. Robinson opened her eyes and glanced at the empty doorway behind me. "My daughter stood in the doorframe behind Maddie. I looked up at her for help, but she was spellbound—frozen in place—as if the devil had turned her dumb. I rubbed Maddie's back, trying desperately to soothe her." Anguish had taken hold of Mrs. Robinson's face at that moment, reliving the memory. She looked down, her white hair barely being held by the clip that slumped to the nape of her neck.

"Shock froze Ruby's face. When she finally snapped out of it, she said Maddie's name. My granddaughter, red in the face and covered in tears—oh how I wished I could get rid of those tears!—she looked up at her mother. My daughter stuttered. 'It's not...' she managed to get out but wasn't able to finish the question. Maddie only buried her head in her arms; shame seemed to smother her as she tried to hide.

"I could only place my hand on her head," Mrs. Robinson explained, giving her raw thumb a break and looked at the empty chair to her left. "I didn't understand any of it," she admitted. "Ruby dragged herself to that chair, right there and fell into it. The weight of the world seemed to press down on her. She stared, dumbfounded, at nothing. She only said two words, but those two words brought a world of havoc to her."

Mrs. Robinson took a tissue to her face and blew her nose. For the first time she looked up at me, as if she was surprised I was still there. Looking away, she continued, "She said that the baby was..." Mrs. Robinson trailed off, her eyes falling to and empty spot on the other side of the room. My nosey Alton blood coursed through my body, angry with the suspense. It thumped in my ears, urging me to ask questions. I refused, holding my tongue and biting my lip, knowing Mrs. Robinson was delicately balancing between reality and a mental breakdown.

Moments passed like a snail on a dry sidewalk. I started to tell myself I wouldn't hear anymore—that Mrs. Robinson had gone into shock, that she was struck by deafening grief. I wondered who I should call to take care of her. Everyone she loved was gone. It was up to her.

I took a deep breath and moved to touch her arm reassuringly; to ask her what I could do. Abruptly she turned to me with such aggressiveness, for a moment I thought she was possessed by something evil. "It was Nate's," she said upset, as if I'd beaten it out of her.

"Ruby said it was Nate's baby," she repeated and a fresh river of tears broke through the wrinkles in her face.

Chapter Twenty-Four

"MADDIE WAS PREGNANT WITH HER FATHER'S CHILD?" I asked, struggling to make the words form. I could hardly wrap my mind around the fact that a story like this was reality in Alton Oaks.

Mrs. Robinson nodded as her eyebrows came together painfully. She dabbed a tissue to her eyes. "Just like her mother."

My eyes studied the counter as I tried to understand the fact that Maddie and Ruby were mother and daughter *and* sisters, and that Maddie's child would also be her aunt and her mother's sibling as well as a grandchild. My head spun with the image of such a tangled family tree.

"I couldn't let that happen," Mrs. Robinson said, her voice turning to stone. "As much as my heart loved the idea of Maddie becoming a mother, I couldn't let it happen this way. I didn't want to see her stuck in the life her mother had. I remembered Mrs. Zaborsky said her daughter-in-law lost her baby when she took too many prescriptions when she'd herniated her back. I immediately went for Greg's medicine cabinet and knew what I had to do.

I sent Ruby home, telling her I'd watch Maddie

that night—that we'd stay in the loft. I had a large breakfast order for the Women's Group in the morning, so I planned on staying anyway," Mrs. Robinson explained as if it had all made sense in her head. "I crushed up some Tramadol and Norco in her hot chocolate—a dash of peppermint oil masks the taste; I learned that years ago. Then I had some Vicodin that I crushed into a powder to calm Greg down and mixed it with the powdered sugar on her pumpkin bread. She was out in no time," she admitted and confusion deepened the lines around her eyes.

"I thought if I kept it up for a few days, the baby would abort itself. I could keep her in my care for a few days, easily. Saturday I kept her in a stupor and kept praying to see blood in the toilet. Everything was going according to plan. Except... well, I didn't even know she'd disappeared in the middle of the night. When I woke up to turn the ovens on downstairs and fulfill the Women's Group order, I swear I saw Maddie on the sofa. I swear she was under the blankets... but it was so dark. Maybe it was all in my mind that I saw the pile of blankets move when I tripped over her backpack and banged my shoulder into the door frame.

"I was going to let her sleep and come back in a few hours with some gingerbread and a fresh cup of cocoa. But the store got so busy with people stopping in for a pastry or doughnut on their way to the Polar Plunge, I didn't get the chance. I didn't even know she was missing until Mrs. Fredrickson stumbled in, her lips still blue from the freezing cold water.

"And I can't help but think I did it," Mrs. Robinson admitted. "It's all my fault."

My head was spinning with the information I was gleaning. Nothing else in the world seemed to exist but this room in the bakery, Mrs. Robinson, and me. "I encouraged Greg to spend time with Ruby when she was younger. I covered up the truth of Ruby's pregnancy—I denied it. And I ultimately killed my granddaughter for being a victim of her father's cruel and unchristian ways. It all started with me."

Chapter Twenty-Five

MY FEET COULDN'T CARRY ME fast enough over the snowbanks and across the street to the police station. I'd gotten up and left Mrs. Robinson without saying a word. She sat unmoving in that metal folding chair, staring at the metallic table top—even her hands were still, limp in her lap as she slouched over with feelings I couldn't begin to fathom.

I wanted to tell Jake everything. And despite everything I'd learned, I wanted Mrs. Robinson's pain to subside. I wanted someone to help her.

Breezing past the swinging wooden gate, the officer at the front desk didn't even bother stopping me. He went back to the game of solitaire on the computer screen that I could see reflected in his smudged eyeglasses. Jake's desk was empty, so I walked past to Chief Gomes' office. It too was empty. Where was everybody?

My eyes travelled to the conference room door, which was closed. I bit my lip and weighed my options. "Hey, Charli! Happy holidays," Seth said, walking up behind me as he sucked on a candy cane. He was an old classmate and always talked to me like a friend, not like a distant stranger which was closer to the truth.

"Hey, Seth," I said, still eyeing the conference room door. "I need to speak to Jake or someone about Maddie's case."

"Oh?" he asked, leaning on the edge of a nearby desk and pulling the candy cane from his mouth. "What about?"

The station wasn't busy, but I looked around nervously. "I was just talking to Mrs. Robinson," I admitted.

"That poor woman," Seth said, shaking his head and biting off a piece of the candy cane. I heard it crunch between his teeth before he continued, "Her whole family's in custody or deceased," he said sadly.

"Right," I said, wanting to skip to the point. "She drugged Maddie the night she was killed."

The crunching of the candy cane stopped mid-bite and his usually happy-go-lucky features turned serious. "What do you mean, 'drugged?'" he asked.

"I mean she wanted to abort the baby so she gave Maddie a bunch of prescription drugs," I shared, wishing the world would start moving in fast-forward. Getting this information into the right hands seemed to be taking forever.

"Baby?" he asked. His eyebrows arched and I could see the thoughts flying behind his eyes. He picked up the phone at the desk beside him. "It's Seth," he said. "I have some tips on the case." There were a few moments of silence before he responded, "Yes," and looked up at me. "Yes" he said again into the phone. "Outside your office," he shared and nervously tapped the corner of the desk. "Charli Parker," he seemed to mumble and I could feel my face flush. "Okay," he finally said and hung up the phone. "Wait here, Charli," he said and then Seth disappeared behind the wooden partition to the front desk.

Chief Gomes lumbered out of the conference room with a sigh that I could hear from the other end of the station. "Get in here," he said as he walked past me, motioning me into his office with a chubby finger.

When Chief Gomes motioned for me to sit down, my leg started shaking with nervousness. I knew Chief Gomes was fair, but he was also stern. I had a feeling he thought I overstepped boundaries when it came to police work.

"What is this I hear about you having information about the case? We just left you at the bakery. What could have possibly happened between then and now?" he asked, a hint of irritation seeping between his words.

"Mrs. Robinson," I said meekly, picking at the worn patch on my jeans, where a hole was starting to form. "Someone needs to talk to her, immediately," I shared.

"The poor woman is going through enough," Chief Gomes said, dismissively.

"That might be very true," I agreed, working up the courage it took to look Chief Gomes in the eye. "But she just told me how she drugged Maddie the night before the Polar Plunge. She wanted to abort the baby—"

"—How do you know about the baby?" he asked, shocked. His eyes swept past me and surveyed the station from his large office window.

I leaned forward in my chair, frustrated that he didn't seem to be hearing me. "Mrs. Robinson told me," I repeated.

"Why would she want to cause harm to her granddaughter? Her great-grandchild? She's the sweetest woman I know. It doesn't make any sense, Charli. She's in shock."

I bit my lip and my eyes traced the elaborate design a pile of rubber bands made in the corner of his desk. "She's a genuinely sweet woman," I agreed. "She didn't want Maddie to have the same life as her daughter."

I bravely glanced at Chief Gomes to gauge his expression. His bushy white eyebrows were unimpressed with the information I'd offered and his hand stroked the milky white beard below his chin. I couldn't hold it in any longer; I spit it out: "Maddie's biological father is Mr. Robinson—Greg. The father of Maddie's child is Nate—her dad."

Chief Gomes' face was stoic as he continued to stroke his beard. I knew it sounded like a wild rumor that would have been overheard at The Buzz. "Mrs. Robinson told me all of this. I swear it! Her world is falling apart. Someone needs to go to the bakery right now," I urged, looking him in the eye, pleading for help.

"Oh hell," he muttered, pushing himself off his chair. "This case is turning into a circus," he remarked as he pulled on his coat. "Go on, get home, Charli," he said almost overwhelmed.

Before he ushered me out of his office with an impatient hand, his voice turned softer and he added, "You've been through enough as well."

Chapter Twenty-Six

THE SUN WAS SHINING AGAINST the icicles on the awnings of the stores on Main Street, melting them in the warmth of the midday light. I didn't want to go back to the Alton House just yet. I needed a dose of brightness before I went back to my musty old bedroom. Sadie's apartment was only a few minutes away, and she encouraged me to use it whenever I needed to since she practically lived at my brother's house anyway.

The closer I got to the corner of Oak and Main, the more I yearned to sit in silence in her apartment—to possibly get lost in binge watching some drama on television. I turned the key over in my hand as it sat deep on my pocket, blocked from the wind racing across the parking lot of Prescott's Grocers.

Sadie's apartment always smelled of peaches and cream—the scented and unburned tea light candles sat on a decorative wall hanging of the Eiffel Tower near the entryway. I took a deep breath and peeled off the warm layers of clothes.

I fell over the back of the red plush couch and draped my arm over my eyes, relishing the stillness of the world. After everything I'd just learned, I needed the world to be still for a few moments. The wind whistled periodically as it grazed the screen on the patio door, and I heard car doors slam in the parking lot outside. I must've dozed off because my eyes shot open to the door banging shut.

"You're here!" Sadie exclaimed brightly. She took off her red pea coat but left on the black beret as she bounded towards me. "Have you heard?" she asked enthusiastically, her eyes bright with gossip.

"Heard what?" I asked. My voice was raspy with sleep as I sat up.

"Mrs. Robinson!" she exclaimed. I braced myself for information I already knew—information I'm sure a nosey citizen overheard me tell Seth at the station. "The poor woman," Sadie said, her features sinking as she shook her head.

I nodded. "Poor woman," I repeated in agreement.

"I just went by the bakery—I was volunteering at the Snow Social and walked past. There was an ambulance on Main Street and Chief Gomes was outside blocking anyone from going in," Sadie said as she took off her beret and threw it on the coffee table.

"An ambulance?" I asked, confused.

Sadie nodded. "They rushed Mrs. Robinson to the hospital."

"What for?" I asked. I could feel my heart beginning to race with the news.

"I called a friend at the hospital—do you remember Donna? No matter—apparently she OD'ed and the chief found her half dead on the floor of the store." Sadie paused and shook her head while looking at her black and white carpet. "I can't imagine what it must be like for her: losing her granddaughter, her daughter is under suspicion of murder, and her husband and son-in-law are in custody for whatever it was they did—I doubt it was setting the store on fire which is what Liza Coperski is telling everyone."

"She's all alone," I said, sadly. The words seemed to pinch my heart.

"Anyway," Sadie said, changing her tone. "I'm getting ready for the Holiday Hop. Alex made a reservation with your dad at Oakie's. Wanna help me?" she asked brightly.

"Sure," I said with a nod, wondering if a distraction was what I needed.

Sadie jumped up from the couch in delight. Her fingers jabbed a few buttons on the decades-old stereo she kept on a black metal baker's rack that had never seen a kitchen. The sides of the shelf had metal ribbons bent into wispy hearts that held old concert lanyards. Upbeat Christmas music began streaming through her apartment and my nerves seemed to settle a little.

"Oh!" she exclaimed and turned to me. "I almost forgot!"

I looked at her questioningly as she bounced to the table in the corner where she kept her laptop and printer, retrieving a brown envelope. "Early Christmas present," she informed and handed it to me. "Just arrived this morning. Priority mail."

"Sadie, you already got me a Christmas present," I protested, realizing that I'd left all my photography supplies at Oakie Doughkie.

Sadie shook her head; her auburn hair bouncing against a sly smile. "You're going to want this present," she said, poking me with the corner of the envelope until I grabbed it.

I sighed and took it from her hands. The envelope was already opened and postmarked from Virginia. Pulling out a bunch of documents, I sat down on the couch and used the coffee table to organize its contents. "It's from Evie,"

Sadie said, sitting beside me. "She found a few things in her research that you might like to see."

As I sorted through the pages, I wondered if Sadie had actually found out why an aged Fort Knox bag was stuffed in the rafters of our attic. This was just the distraction I needed.

I unfolded a large sheet of paper that had the Alton family tree typed out in a spreadsheet. It included me and my siblings and went back several generations. I saw Andrew Alton's name and noticed he was the only child under his father, Joseph Alton. I thought back to the journal entries as my finger brushed their names. No surprises jumped out and I placed it on the table.

Next, there were photocopies of Western Union telegrams—the capture of Tall T, Mad John, and other criminals. Newspaper articles dating back to the turn of the century, mostly explaining the establishment of Alton Oaks and its growth and how and when its boundaries were shaped.

The last item was an old photograph—not photocopied like the rest of the pieces. It was an actual photograph of two men. I knew one was Andrew Alton, though he was young in the photograph. He didn't yet have the wrinkles around his eyes or the mustache he sported in the photograph with his wife and two sons that used to hang in our living room.

The other man was just as tall as Andrew, but with dark hair that was swept back beneath a hat of the times and his eyes were two dark secrets, though his smile was jovial. There was something vaguely familiar about him, but I couldn't place where I'd seen his face before.

"Turn it over," Sadie said, sitting beside me.

There, in fading ink it read: Andrew Alton & Brent Oaks, 1914.

"The town wasn't named after trees," Sadie explained, pointing to the name beside my great-great-grandfather's. "It was named after Andrew Alton and his partner," she added. "And Evie wasn't able to find any record of Brent Oaks in any of her research. None at all. It's like he was wiped out of history."

My stomach churned and I began to bite my thumb, staring at the faces in the photograph. What was history trying to hide? And what did that mean for the Alton family?

Chapter Twenty-Seven

I LEFT SADIE TO PREPARE FOR THE HOLIDAY HOP, as I complained of an upset stomach. I wasn't sure I'd be good company at the Holiday Hop and wondered if Jake could get someone else to go on short notice. As I walked down Main Street, I began to wonder if Andrew Alton wasn't as valiant as I'd made him out to be—did he wipe Brent Oaks from history? Was that why he was murdered? Who was Brent Oaks?

I wound up in Town Circle and I stared up at Town Hall, knowing that those very steps were where Andrew Alton was found dead. The whole town celebrated my great-great-grandfather—his accomplishments, his service to our country, his vision for the town. What happened all those years ago? What secrets were lost to history? What was really behind the Alton family name?

"Are you okay, Charli?"

My head was swimming with so many questions and uncertainties that I didn't hear Jake come up behind me and I jumped. "I saw you standing there as I left the police station and called your name," he explained.

"Sorry," I said, shaking my head. "Just a lot of stuff inside my head right now."

"Sometimes a good walk helps," he said, nodding towards the canal trail. "I needed to step out and clear my head too," he admitted.

Not many people were walking along the canal trail at sunset, though it was only four o'clock in the afternoon. The nights were cold, especially when there were no clouds in the sky. "You meant what you said, about keeping confidence, right?" Jake said suddenly.

I watched my breath come out in a cloud as I nodded. "Sometimes it just helps to talk these things out," he said, turning up his collar against the wind.

He was offering me a distraction and I felt a rush of gratitude for it. "This case is taking too many turns. It's like a maze without an end," he admitted. "We're waiting on DNA results to see if the rumors about paternity are true," he shared.

"If the rumors are true, does that give him motive?" I asked and shivered when Nate's face crossed my mind.

"It could," Jake said, shrugging indifferently. "Especially if Nate doesn't want anybody to know."

"You don't think so?" I asked, studying the way Jake's eyes squinted as we passed a lamp post along the path.

"What I think doesn't matter," he said. "What matters are the facts."

I remember him telling me this line more than once in the past eight months. I liked that he was always confident in his abilities as a police officer. I nodded in response. "Yes, but instinct is important too."

"My instinct is that there's something wrong with Nate, but I need facts to tell me what it is," he said, frustrated. I understood why he needed a walk to clear his head.

We walked for several moments in silence. "I don't like these dark corners of Alton Oaks that are coming to light," I admitted. "I miss the way things used to be." I thought back to my childhood on these streets. I missed the friendships, the naivety, the innocence. The life I experienced here before my grown-up eyes came to Alton Oaks.

Jake didn't respond. He only scratched his chin as we walked.

"Do you think Maddie could've accidentally fallen in?" I asked. "She sounded pretty drugged up." Maybe, for once in this town's string of unfortunate events, this death was merely an accident."

Jake didn't confirm or deny the question; he was still stuck on facts. "Without knowing what happened between the bakery and where she turned up at the Polar Plunge, there's no answer. It's a possibility, of course."

"And everyone has an alibi?" I asked.

"Not iron-clad ones. Everyone claimed to be sleeping. Mrs. Robinson was sleeping in the loft. Mr. Robinson was at home. Ruby was asleep in her own bed in Terryville with Nate asleep on his recliner in the living room."

There was a long pause with only the sound of a snow mobile somewhere in the trees. Finally, Jake said, "I don't know if this one's going to be solved, Charli. There're too many unknowns; not enough facts."

At that moment, I had the urge to tell him he was the best detective since Columbo; that if anybody would solve this case it would be him. Playing to his ego would have been something I would have done with Jackson, but Jake was different. I wasn't there to inflate his self-esteem, I was there to be a friend; to help.

"You've surveyed the area between the bakery and the river, I assume?" I asked instead.

"Of course, we did," he said incredulously. "With all the tracks from the Polar Plunge and the newly fallen snow, there was nothing to find.

"We also talked to store owners and citizens to see if anyone saw anything that night, but between 10:30 and 1:30, nothing was open," he added.

"Well, nothing but the library," I said.

Jake looked at me quizzically.

"The Winter Reading Lock-In was happening all night. My mom was there with about fifty students and two dozen chaperones," I explained.

"We asked the staff if they saw anything that night—anything out of the ordinary—but they didn't—and you *know* your mom," Jake pointed out. "If she saw something, the whole town would know about it."

"She might not have seen anything," I shared, "but there are a lot of windows in that library, maybe—"

"—Maybe a kid saw something," we said in unison.

"Charli, you're amazing!" Jake said and spun around, starting to jog towards Town Circle. He stopped a few yards away and asked, "Well, are you coming with me?"

I smiled at his invitation and my snow boots pounded against the frozen pavement to catch up with him.

Chapter Twenty-Eight

THE LIBRARY WAS CLOSING IN TWENTY MINUTES when we arrived. The large wooden circulation desk sat guarding the entrance and the woman I met at the tree lighting ceremony—Wanda? Harriet? I could never remember!—sat behind the desk in a Santa hat and a festive green sweater. "Charli! Happy holidays! I'm glad to see you visiting the library!" she exclaimed in a hushed whisper. "And you brought a friend! Here, have a candy cane bookmark," she encouraged, sliding the container of bookmarks towards us.

"Thanks." I smiled quickly, but neglected to pick up a bookmark. Instead, my gloved hand gripped the wooden ledge between us. "Is my mother still here?"

The woman smiled and her snowman-themed earrings bobbed as she nodded. "Yes. I believe she's in the back. You go ahead on back."

Jake was at my heels as we zipped past the stacks. An elderly gentleman was sitting in a cushioned chair reading a newspaper and a teenager was hunched over a notebook with a pile of books teetering beside her. We went through the door marked 'Employees Only' without a second thought.

The southeast corner of the room had four cubicles and my mother's desk was closest to us. She picked her head up from the computer screen with our abrupt presence. "Charli!" she lit up. "What are you doing here?" she asked, embracing me in a hug. I felt like I hadn't seen her in days. "And Jake, what brings you here?" Her face suddenly drained of color. "Am I under arrest? I swear I didn't do anything." With me being under suspicion of murder during the summer and my sister getting thrown into the murder of my husband, I didn't blame my mother for her reaction.

"No, Mrs. Parker," Jake said good-humoredly. "You're not under arrest."

"Good," she said. Her features relaxed and she sat back in her chair.

"I need to ask you about the Winter Reading Lock-In," Jake said, pulling up the closest chair to be eye level with my mother.

"Oh, it was the best one yet!" my mother exclaimed, glowing. "Fifty-two participants! It was the first year the all-night read aloud lasted the entire night! Do you know how many pages were read that night, cumulatively?"

"Actually," Jake said, cutting into my mother's boasting. "I need to know if any of the participants saw anything strange. If the students saw anything."

"No one said anything," my mother informed. "Actually, I did think of something odd that happened."

"Odd?" Jake asked.

My mother nodded. "When we gave the students pizza around 9:45 or so, I did a head count while other chaperones checked their assigned area for any students. I have my chaperones radio me with a head count every hour on the hour throughout the night," she informed.

Jake nodded, understanding.

"At 10:00, I counted all fifty-two participants outside here, at the tables where we served the pizza." My mother pointed to the door we'd walked through minutes ago. "The strange thing was that Mrs. Reynolds radioed that she had a student asleep at the private study tables upstairs. It turned out she wasn't a participant but was studying and fell asleep before the library closed for the lock-in. We woke her up and unlocked the door to let her go home."

"What was this student's name?" Jake asked, taking out his Steno pad from his jacket pocket.

My mom's eyes squinted as she tried to pull the name from her memory. "Wendy. Wendy something. Hold on; I have it written down somewhere," she said as she began sifting through papers and post-it notes on her desk.

"Wendy Nottingham?" Jake asked.

"Yes!" My mom said, nodding, as she pulled the yellow post-it note from the corner of her desk. "How did you know?"

Jake turned to look at me, knowing he had a new lead, one we didn't see coming.

Excusing himself, he walked to the corner of the room to radio the station. "What is it?" my mom asked me as I sat in the seat Jake had vacated. I hesitated to give her more information. "This has to do with Maddie's death, doesn't it?" she asked, digging for information.

I nodded and bit my thumbnail.

"Don't do that, Charli," my mother said, pulling my hand from my mouth. I sighed dramatically in response.

Suddenly my mother's features froze and her eyes focused on the dated Reading Rainbow poster on the wall behind me. "What is it, Mom?" I asked. My mind automatically went to the heart attack she'd had on Thanksgiving a few years ago and panic began to build as

I leaned forward.

Her eyes drifted to me with realization. "It's the same Wendy who was battling Maddie for valedictorian, isn't it?" she asked.

I nodded, searching her eyes for signs of distress. "Charli," she breathed. "Wendy's just outside this door."

Chapter Twenty-Nine

JAKE AND I LEFT MY MOTHER in the backroom as we tentatively snuck a glance into the study area. I knew my mother's nose would peek out of the door as soon as we exited. I wouldn't doubt she'd picked up her cell phone to text Mrs. Kratsky as soon as our backs were turned.

"Come with me," Jake instructed, though I'm sure he meant it as a suggestion rather than a command.

I nodded.

"You tend to lend a calming presence to people," he said passively. Honestly, I was beginning to think I might be made of a truth serum—some type of kryptonite. People were telling me things I didn't want to know—my conversation with Mrs. Robinson, for example. A shiver went down my spine at the thought of the horrors she'd told me.

Jake's winter jacket, complete with the Alton Oaks emblem embroidered on the sleeve, made a swishy sound as we walked. It seemed too loud for the library. We both reached the other side of the table where Wendy was sitting and she didn't take notice. A fortress of books lay open around her as she scribbled notes into a ragged notebook.

"Wendy?" Jake asked in a tone above a whisper. An elderly gentleman turned a page of his newspaper and glanced in our direction.

The blue pen that had been frantically scribbling stopped, but Wendy didn't look up. Before I could greet her, she jumped out of her chair and dashed out the front door. I turned to Jake, confused, but he took off after her. Grabbing the young girl's jacket from the back of her chair, I chased after both of them.

The library was at the end of Main Street. Wendy either had to take off downtown—where people were still doing last minute Christmas shopping—or run down the mostly deserted path by the river. When I bolted out of the library doors, I took a chance that I'd find them on the bike path, since there was no sign of them beneath the bright entry lights of the library doors.

"No one will ever believe me!" I heard a girl yell desperately a few yards away. I could just make out two figures under a lamp post on the path. Wendy had slipped on a patch of ice and Jake had caught up with her.

"There's nothing I can tell you to make you believe me. Everyone will always think it was me!" she yelled through hysterical tears as I caught up to them.

"Why do you say that?" Jake asked. His breath was coming out in puffs in the chilly night air.

Wendy only sobbed without speaking, sinking onto the cold concrete.

I walked past Jake and crouched down beside the distressed girl. I draped her coat over her shoulders as the biting chill began to pierce its claws into my exposed skin. "Wendy, what happened?" I asked.

Angrily, Wendy admitted, "I came across Maddie on this path. The night she died." She took a deep breath and added, "There! I said it! Now everyone will think it was me. No matter what I say it won't change their minds!"

I kept a hand on Wendy's shoulder as she cried. It must've been a secret that weighed heavily on her. Releasing it must have brought a sense of condemnation and confusing relief. I glanced at Jake, but he clearly left this situation up to me as he kept his respectful distance.

I squeezed Wendy's shoulder and sat down on the cold concrete beside her. "She was out of it—no one will believe me! I was just walking home. I fell asleep at the library and thought it'd be faster to go home through the woods by Gnarled Circle Drive," she admitted through hands that covered her tear-streaked face.

I was familiar with this path as Sadie had grown up in that well-to-do part of Alton Oaks. We'd often take this short cut home from school as the Alton House was on the other side of the woods from Gnarled Circle Drive. It was a faster route than walking up Oak Street.

"I didn't understand what she was saying. She was just out wandering. I thought maybe she was sleepwalking. I tried talking to her but the only thing I could make out was 'I gotta get away,' but she kept mumbling nonsense." Wendy paused and wiped her nose with the sleeve of her sweater. I adjusted her coat as it slipped from her shoulders.

"It was so cold out that night," she continued. "I tried to take her hand—to take her back to town for help. It was too dark on the path. She pulled away and stumbled off. I tried so hard to stop her!" Wendy broke down into a sob again. "I really did try. No one will ever believe me. They'll think I pushed her into the river so I could become valedictorian. No one will ever believe me! I really did try to help!"

I looked up at Jake. He looked skeptical and rubbed his chin with his gloved hand. "What exactly happened,

Wendy?" I asked.

"Well, I wasn't going to leave her there, was I?" Wendy snapped. She rose from the ground and slipped her arms into her jacket. "Not the way she was acting. I tried to pull her back to town. I tried so hard! I pulled on her backpack and her coat. I thought about holding onto her legs, but then she kicked me in the crotch, which was weird. It didn't hurt as much as if I were a boy, but I let go of her and she took off down the path, into the dark.

"I ran after her. I called her name. She just disappeared," Wendy said, looking into the shadows that lined the path. The glimpse of hope in her eyes was unmistakable; as if Maddie might walk onto the path at any minute. "If I'd known what had happened, I would've called for help. I would have done something."

"Why didn't you call for help? Tell someone about it?" Jake asked.

Wendy wiped her nose again with her sleeve and hugged her chest. "Because I walked up and down the path for almost two hours looking for her, but saw no trace of her. Nothing. Not a soul. Not a sound," she explained, grief and desperation dusting her tone.

"I went back to Town Circle and saw the light on in the loft at the bakery. I assumed she went there, since she lives in Terryville and the buses weren't running. It was late and I didn'et want to make anyone worry at one in the morning if Maddie was safe at the bakery. I was going to check in with her at the bakery the next morning—I swear it!" she exclaimed. "Only," she looked down, "by then Maddie was found."

"Why didn't you say anything then?" Jake asked, stepping closer.

"Who'd believe me?" Wendy asked, looking squarely at Jake. "No one! Maddie and I were always neck-and-neck for valedictorian. Everyone at school made our rivalry seem like this big Joker and Batman feud. I didn't kill her. I didn't need to say anything."

Before Jake could ask a follow-up question, I inquired, "Wendy, what time did you come across Maddie that night?"

She bit her bottom lip and her eyes dragged across the bare tree limbs above us. "I left the library just before half-past, so I must've come across Maddie at 10:30. I struggled with her for what seemed like forever. I tried," she said, her eyes pleading with us, bouncing between Jake and me. "I really did."

A strong breeze steamrolled down the path, carrying bits of snow that stung our faces. "Wendy," Jake started, "I need you to come to the station and call your parents."

Tears immediately began welling up in her eyes. "I swear I didn't kill her!" she exclaimed hysterically. "I swear it! I could never hurt her! I admired her! She was always so focused! She was always so good! No matter what! I really didn't do anything! I don't care about being valedictorian!"

Jake looked at me for help; I guess he didn't know how to deal with a hysterical teenager.

"Wendy," I said, stepping in. "I believe you," I said genuinely and knew that Jake couldn't. "But you're seventeen. You need your parents here to help you. You need to pull yourself together to get through this. Okay?"

Wendy wiped her tears and nodded. "Okay," she said.

I glanced at Jake and he nodded with gratitude as I led Wendy back down the path to Town Circle.

Chapter Thirty

WHEN I FINALLY MADE IT HOME, two hours later, I took an aspirin for a headache that was starting, and hungrily drank a can of chicken noodle soup before retiring to my bedroom. The only thing I really wanted to do was sit in my quiet, dark room and edit some of the pictures I'd taken for Mrs. Lupizo's photography project.

Not long after I closed my bedroom door, I heard Christmas music playing and my nephew singing his own lyrics to "Rudolph the Red-Nosed Reindeer."

"Charli!" my mother called up from the bottom of the staircase. "Pumpkin pie?"

I knew Carter was at the fire station. It was day two of his three-day shift, which meant Bailey was always over at the house. "No!" I yelled and hoped that answer would suffice. My mother would be wanting to know more about what had happened with Wendy, but I didn't want to be social at the moment.

It only took a few more moments before the doorbell rang and Bailey's voice called from the bottom of the stairs, "Charli! Door!"

Rubbing my eyes, already tired from looking at a screen, I groaned. Tightening the drawstring on my sweats,

I yelled, "Coming!" as I slipped into a pair of old moccasins.

As I bounded down the stairs, I saw Jake in the foyer. The flashing Christmas lights from outside the windows illuminated him. "I know I'm late," he said. "Interesting fashion choice," he added, eyeing my sweatpants and an oversized hoodie that I'd stolen from Alex's closet when he and Sadie had hosted a bonfire in their backyard during Halloween.

It hit me that the Holiday Hop was tonight! It had been such a long day that I'd forgotten. "I thought you were working," I said, noticing that the house was abnormally quiet.

"I was," he said, shifting his feet. The idea of not being at work right now obviously made him uneasy, but he tried to mask it. "But it's the *Holiday Hop,*" he said, and I knew what he meant; when would we ever get the chance to go to the Holiday Hop again without spending hundreds of dollars on a ticket? "What are you waiting for? Go grab your camera!" he said with an encouraging smile.

"Jake, I can't go. Not like this." I motioned to my greasy hair that was knotted on the top of my head. My eyes were undoubtedly red and glassy from staring at the computer screen in the dark. The Holiday Hop was an event where everyone dressed to the nines; it was like prom for small town adults with money to burn.

"I'm a fan of the grungy, just rolled-out-of-bed look you've got going on, but I'll wait if you'd rather go put on something more traditional." Jake smiled and then added, "I have a pair of blue sweatpants at home that I can change into, if you'd rather we match."

I smiled at his humor. Just then Bailey poked her head from around the corner of the living room and exclaimed, "No sister of mine is going to the Holiday Hop in sweatpants!"

She automatically grabbed my hand as if to chastise me and thrust my snow boots into my arms. "You wait here," she instructed Jake. "Twenty minutes," she added and then pulled me out the front door before I could fasten my boots.

Without arguing, I let Bailey use a variety of sprays from her crowded bathroom closet to make my hair look fresh and clean in a quick but surprisingly elegant updo. She hand-picked a silvery white dress she'd worn to the Fireman's Ball in the past, and pulled out a pair of icy blue heels from a box deep in her walk-in closet. She worked with barely a word and for the first time in years, Bailey and I were in the same room for more than ten minutes without arguing. I obeyed as she gave me instructions: hold this, lift this, breathe in, stand still, hold your breath.

It had only taken thirty minutes for Bailey to return me to her front yard, where Jake was sitting in his green 1999 Subaru Imprezza, my camera bag in the passenger seat. I hadn't seen that car since high school. "You still drive this thing?" I asked, slipping into the warm passenger seat. Though Jake and I rarely talked in high school, I would always notice this car parked in his driveway when I got off the school bus. The car smelled like new leather instead of two decades of garage fumes.

Jake shrugged. "My parents kept it for some reason," he explained, backing out of the driveway. "I think the upkeep kept my dad busy until my mom could retire. It sits in the garage until I have to go out of town or to the airport."

"I've never been in this car before," I stated, looking at how clean and dustless it was.

"Never?" Jake asked. His eyes didn't leave the road as

he navigated through the ruts in the snow.

I shook my head. The radio was low and tuned to the station that played Christmas music. The soothing voice of Bing Crosby no longer made me think of old movies, but of the Oakie Doughkie bakery. I shivered and hoped I didn't have to return to the store to photograph ever again.

"Is it too cold?" Jake asked, adjusting the knobs on the dashboard.

"No, it's fine," I said, resigned. "I was just thinking of..." I trailed off and thought not to ruin the night with unpleasant topics. "Never mind."

Jake's hair was combed slightly to the side—a sign that he needed a haircut; his hair was normally too short to comb. The light from the street lamps on Oak & Main illuminated his raised eyebrows. "Thinking of what?" he pressed.

I sighed and ran my fingers over the velvet-like material that Bailey's dress was made from. "The store. How Christmas isn't Christmas anymore," I said. Christmas in Alton Oaks was always so whimsical. It was something I daydreamed about in the sub-tropic climate of Costa Rica, or during the snowless, sunny days in Albuquerque. Christmas in my hometown was full of warm hugs, smiles over mugs of hot cocoa, and that anticipation of Christmas morning filling each day. It wasn't like that anymore.

Jake nodded as the snow-covered decorations of downtown Alton Oaks filled the rearview mirrors. "I get it," he said. "Christmas stopped being Christmas a few years ago."

"Why do you think that is?" I asked. I thought I'd never stop being the person who decorated for Christmas as soon as Thanksgiving dinner was over. Jackson hated that.

Jake shrugged as the street lamps disappeared and the dark sky revealed the stars. The hospital was two miles up the road. I hadn't been down this road since Rip and I came across Jesse, half beaten to death, two months ago. So many of my innocent Alton Oaks memories had been tainted since I'd returned home. No longer was my elementary school a whimsical whirlwind of playground memories; now it was full of unpleasant memories of murder and the most unpleasant principal I'd ever known. I couldn't even go to the grocery store without thinking about how I'd been stabbed in the shoulder.

"At least," I started, talking aloud more to myself than to Jake, "Maddie died accidentally. I don't know how many more murders I can take in this town." Alton Oaks was my safe-place; it was why I came back. Since my return, it seems anything but safe. Each crime hurt me personally. I felt a sense of ownership to Alton Oaks—the town founded by my great-great grandfather. I didn't want to see it fall to corruption.

Jake pursed his lips together. "What?" I asked, knowing Jake well enough that he was trying not to speak his mind. "What is it?"

"Something about this case," he admitted.

"What about it?" I asked.

He shook his head. "There's something about it that just bothers me. Like an itch I can't quite reach."

"What do you think it is?"

Jake exhaled loudly as the bright lights of the hospital began to glow in the distance. "I don't know," he admitted.

Chapter Thirty-One

THOUGH THE ATMOSPHERE WAS JUBILANT AND BRIGHT—a quartet of string instruments playing classical versions of Christmas tunes and the smell of cinnamon and balsam fir filling the air—Jake and I walked under the entrance decorated with garland of holly and pinecones with slumped shoulders. The room was filled with men in tuxedos and women in dazzling gowns. Their images were reflected in the mirrors and a dazzling display of icicles dripping from the ceiling. I immediately pulled out my camera and began taking photos.

We walked around the large room, not recognizing any faces. In one corner there were two large fondue fountains near a large bar that three people, dressed in pleated black clothes and red neckties, tended. The same uniformed staff drifted through the crowd with trays of caviar, pâté, escargot, and other fancy appetizers I only knew about from watching the TV show *Frasier* as a kid.

"I feel like an imposter," Jake whispered, leaning over my shoulder.

"I know," I agreed. I tried to look past the facade of costumes and make-up, but I didn't recognize a soul in the room. There was an ocean of judgement in the air and I felt like I was barely staying afloat.

"Deputy Vega," a tall man with a well-groomed white beard said, extending a hand. The word *debonair* defined every inch of him and I smiled in his direction. "Mark Weingarten," he introduced. "I own the Inn; we met over the summer."

"Oh yes," Jake said with the handshakes. The man's aura was domineering, but in an endearing way.

"I can't thank you enough for how well you handled that incident this summer with those Canaries. I'm thankful that woman didn't die in my establishment. Your indiscretion and professionalism has not been forgotten," he added.

"Ah, yes. Well, thank-you," Jake said, tripping over his words. He turned to me, "Have you met Charli Parker?" he asked.

The man's expression faltered, as if he'd been caught in a lie and it confused me as his large, warm, soft hand enveloped mine in a handshake. "I haven't had the pleasure," he said, making direct eye contact. His stare was so potent it made me uncomfortable. "I'm sorry for your loss," he shared, his eyes seeming to search mine for something deeper than recognition and I had to look away.

"Thank you," I muttered, my eyes sweeping the floor. It was uncomfortable knowing that the whole town knew my name through rumors and the newspaper articles surrounding Jackson's death in the autumn. It then struck me that the incident in his hotel that he'd mentioned was when Jessica was found hanging from her belt.

Feeling a bit stifled, I excused myself from the conversation and slipped into the hallway. There were several tall tables with small rosemary plants as centerpieces in the hallway. Placing my camera on an empty one, I stood at one with a glass of water, feeling the chill from the night seeping through the window. "Oh, Claudia, how are you?" I overheard a woman in greeting. I recognized the man whose side she'd left as the head of oncology—Alex had introduced me to him once when I'd met him for lunch in the hospital cafeteria.

The two women exchanged pleasantries and, without hesitation, dove straight into gossip—such was the way in Alton Oaks. "Tragic about that young girl. What was her name? Margaret?" the woman named Claudia commented.

"You know very well her name's Maggie," the other woman said judgmentally.

"That's short for Margaret, isn't it, *Kathleen*?" Claudia asked.

"You know I dislike being referred to by that name," the woman said, her penciled eyebrow rose with imprudence.

Claudia forced a laugh and waved her hand dismissively. "I only jest Kate. But it's horrible news. I heard it was an accident."

"It is," Claudia agreed. "My daughter—you remember Penelope? She has a scholarship to Western, you know—she was on her nightly run on the bike path. She said she overheard Wendy tell the police that Maggie was drunk as a skunk. The girl fell into the river herself."

"What a shame," Kate tskked, shaking her head slightly. "She was on such a straight and narrow path, I hear. Valedictorian, just like my Madison," Kate beamed.

"I've heard that her boyfriend—what was his name? Jordan?—it was his fault, treated her horribly. Just look at that family," Claudia said judgmentally as she took an hors d'oeurve from a passing tray.

Kate took an hors d'oeurve from the same tray and added, "Well, Maggie's family isn't much better. The stories I've heard from the ladies in my book club who live in Terryville are awful. Simply horrific."

"The grandfather—the one who owns the bakery—Mr. Robertson. I thought he'd done it. He's also so brash and angry. A few years ago we'd taken Henry to the bakery one Sunday to buy some cakes for my mother-in-law. Henry—he was about eight years old at the time—knocked over some of products and that man was horrendous. I threatened to call my lawyer."

Kate nodded in agreement, her curled updo didn't budge with the movement. "My little Fiona—she's in fourth grade now, can you believe it? Won the science fair in the fall, too. She said she saw 'the man from the bakery' outside the library that night; scared her half to death!" The woman paused to take a sip of her champagne.

"Fiona's so sharp; she follows in her big sister's footsteps. I wouldn't be surprised if she was valedictorian as well," Kate added smugly. "She was doing the all-night book event at the library. She said she was reading by the fireplace, in that quaint little window seat, and she looked up to see that wretched man out the window. Lord only knows what he was doing! I shudder to think about it! I thought for sure he had something to do with Maggie's demise."

Claudia listened with thin lips. "What was he doing out there in the middle of the night, do you think? Such strange behavior!" she remarked, stirring the olive in her martini glass. Discreetly, I grabbed my camera and focused on her jeweled fingers as they grabbed the glass that reflected the red bows on the rosemary centerpiece.

"Oh lord, I have no idea. I'd rather not think such *uncivilized* thoughts," Kate said snobbishly. "This champagne is making me heady," she added, touching her manicured hands to her forehead.

"That's why I prefer the martinis," Claudia said and

drained her glass.

"I overheard that the Manhattans are extraordinary. Excuse me," Kate said and scurried away from the table.

It was all gossip, and I couldn't even take it to heart when they got both Maddie and Mr. Robinson's names wrong. Still, I debated whether or not to tell Jake and I stirred the ice in my sweating water glass.

"Charli," Jake greeted, nearly making me jump as I was lost in the snow falling outside the tall, dark windows. "There you are."

"Sorry," I apologized. "I was starting to feel..." I let my sentence get away from me as I recalled a memory of when I'd nearly drowned in the river when I was a kid.

"I know," Jake said, leaning his elbow on the table. "He was very uncouth when he spoke about *that incident,*" Jake said, carefully choosing his words.

"Uncouth?" I asked with a smile.

Jake's cheeks seemed to flush. He dismissed my question with a shake of his head. "I realized something when I was talking to Weingarten."

"What's that?" I asked, still smiling from his choice of words.

"The itch I haven't been able to reach," he explained. "Wendy said Maddie was wearing her backpack that night, but it wasn't found on the body. At first I thought maybe it was carried by the river current but Mrs. Robinson—"

The fact hit me too. "Didn't she say she tripped over it on her way to the bakery that morning?" I asked.

Jake smiled. "Exactly," he said, tapping his finger on the white tablecloth as he spoke. "The timeline doesn't match-up. How could it have been on Maddie around 10:30 that night when she disappeared, but still be at the loft at four o'clock in the morning?"

"Unless either Wendy or Mrs. Robinson was lying," I

pointed out.

Or it's lying on the bottom of the river," he said.

"Wherever that backpack is, it's going to give us some answers."

"If someone has that backpack, Jake," I said, looking around and lowering my voice. "They were probably the last one to see Maddie alive."

Chapter Thirty-Two

AS IF A BREEZE OF FRESH AIR CAME and renewed our senses, Jake and I were alight with this new lead. Jake excused himself to call for a search warrant while I managed to take a few photos of the orchestra, illuminated against a backdrop of lights that looked like water melting down icicles. I'd captured the Holiday Hop sign above the boughs that draped the entrance, shadowed silhouettes captured on the wall beside, due to the floor lights that lit the entrance like an elegant landing strip.

"Hey, Charli," Jake said, sidling up beside me. "The judge is faxing a search warrant over to the station. I figured we'd start with the last place in the timeline the backpack was seen: the loft."

"Let's go," I said without skipping a beat. "What are we waiting for?"

Jake smiled in response and we nearly raced to the coat check. We made a short pit-stop at Sadie's apartment so I could change my clothes—I didn't dare show up at the Alton House for fear I'd be bombarded with questions from my mother or my sister who both dreamed of attending the Holiday Hop. Luckily, my inquisitive best friend—'Questions McInquiry' is the endearing nickname

I gave her but wouldn't dare call her that to her face—wasn't home. She was either at Oakies' still eating an extravagant dinner, or somewhere among the crowd at the Holiday Hop.

I threw my sister's dress over Sadie's closet door and kicked the shoes into a corner. Ripping a hoodie from a hanger and pulling a pair of leggings from a nearby drawer, I dressed hastily and squeezed into a pair of snow boots that were a bit snug for my feet. I kept my sister's pea coat, though it didn't provide as much warmth as my parka.

"All ready?" Jake asked, taken aback as I hopped back into the car. "That was incredibly quick."

He put the car in gear and pulled out of the nearly empty Prescott's Grocers' parking lot as I shrugged in response. I began pulling bobby pins from my hair and building a pile of them in my lap as Jake turned onto Main Street. A flood of relief seemed to loosen my shoulders as my hair fell free from the nest my sister had put it in. I pulled all the stray ringlets into a pony tail and exhaled as if returning home from a long trip.

"Aren't you going to change?" I asked as he drove past Oak Street and pulled into a parking spot near the police station.

He shook his head dismissively as he put the car into park. "I have a change of clothes in my locker. I wonder how long we'll have to wait for the search warrant," he mused as he unbuckled.

I did the same and followed him out of the car. "Hey, Vega!" an officer I recognized but didn't know greeted, coming up to Jake as he crossed the wooden partition. "Didja lose a bet?" he asked with a smile, eyeing Jake's shiny shoes and fancy attire.

"Kapersky," Jake greeted coldly. "Any news on the

warrant?"

"No," he said, following us to Jake's desk. "I'm Damian," he said, extending a hand to me.

I shook it without much enthusiasm. "Charli," I responded.

He nodded playfully and said, "I know. We kinda met in the corn field in October, but it wasn't the place to—"

"Are Robinson and Prince in the cell or the conference room?" Jake asked, cutting him off. He took off his jacket and placed it on the back of his desk chair.

"Neither," Damian responded and shook his head. "They were released about an hour ago. We also got an update on Mrs. Robinson: her stomach's been pumped. She's in recovery but unconscious."

"And the young girl, Wendy. Has she gone?" Jake asked, checking a file that was on his desk.

"Not fifteen minutes ago," Damian reported.

"Okay," Jake said, checking his phone. "Keep me updated."

Damian gave a juvenile salute in response and turned. As he walked away, Jake pointed to the chair beside his desk. "Wait here. I'll be right back." His face softened as if he remembered he wasn't talking to Damian anymore. He pointed to his tuxedo and rolled his eyes. I watched him disappear behind another door that I assumed led to the locker room.

The police station was drafty and I pulled the pea coat closer as I sat down. Not two seconds after Jake closed the door behind him, Damian wheeled himself next to me in one long, swift motion on his office chair. "So," he said in a long, drawn out syllable.

I raised my eyebrows in response.

"You and Vega, huh?" he asked, leaning on the arm rest dramatically and spun around to face me. He looked me up and down as if assessing my worth.

Again, I raised my eyebrows in question.

"Okay, keep quiet. That's fine," he said as if my body language was telling a different story. "I'm like Miss Muffet," he said and leaned his head towards me as if we were conspiring. "I have curds *and* ways to get information."

I wasn't sure I could lift my eyebrows any higher, so I opened my mouth to respond, but had no idea where to start.

"Kapersky!" Jake snapped, approaching the desk while rolling up his long-sleeved plaid shirt. I was surprised he was wearing civilian clothes instead of changing into his uniform.

Damian turned in his chair slowly and lifted a Manila envelope. "Just thought you'd like to know that I found this search warrant in the fax machine," he responded.

Jake grabbed it from his hands. Opening the envelope, he only took a few seconds to read its contents and I saw his eyes light up. He reached for his jacket and turned to me. "Ready?"

I nodded, eager to leave Damian's strange gaze.

Public Works employees were shoveling and salting the new fallen snow from the downtown sidewalks. Flashing lights of the plows reflected in the dark windows of the nearby stores as they drove down Main Street.

Jake hastily made his way to the end of the block where snow banks weren't blocking the streets. "Have you ever been in the loft?" Jake asked as we carefully crossed the slippery road.

"No," I said, shaking my head. I pulled the hood from Sadie's sweater over my head and wished I had my parka... or at least a pair of gloves. "But I know you can enter from the store and from the alley," I shared, remembering the wooden staircase that zig-zagged up the back of the building.

Jake didn't respond. Instead he led me down to the alley and we walked shoulder-to-shoulder in the cold shadows before the motion-sensor flood lights behind the stores began popping to life with our movement.

The wooden stairs hadn't been shoveled in at least a month, I assessed. There was a hard, frozen layer of snow beneath the fresh snowflakes. I had to hold onto the snow-covered railing, slipping more than once as I climbed them in a pair of knee-high boots from Sadie's closet. As I slipped for the tenth time, I could hear Sadie's voice in my head as my heart pumped with the swear words I held in: "What they lack in traction and warmth they totally make up for in fashion," and I rolled my eyes.

"You okay?" Jake would ask every time I slid and grasped the wooden railing tighter with my frozen hands to balance myself.

"Uh-huh," I managed to say as we rounded the last short flight of stairs.

A few stairs behind Jake, I watched him knock on the door as I precariously climbed the last five stairs. "This is Deputy Vega with the police department," he announced. We both knew no one was there, but I assumed he was following some kind of rules. "I have a warrant to search the premises."

Without skipping a beat, Jake got down on one knee and pulled something out of his pocket. "What are you doing?" I asked, stepping onto the small four-foot by four-foot square porch.

"Picking the lock," he said, concentrating on the task.

"Is that legal?" I asked.

He paused, turned to me amused, and responded. "I

could kick the door in, if you prefer. But I find it very rude."

Do they teach you to do that in police-school?" I asked, leaning over his shoulder and blocking the little light he had.

"The academy," he corrected and turned the knob on the door. Slightly amazed at this skill, I followed him into the dark loft. It was the size of the bakery. The entryway led into the kitchen and spilled out into the living room/bedroom studio. A small door immediately to our left led into a diminutive bathroom and Jake automatically checked first—even pushing aside the plain white, no-nonsense shower curtain.

Handing me a pair of gloves from his pocket, he instructed, "Put these on but try not to touch anything. Look for a backpack."

I nodded and quickly put my hands in the gloves, hoping they'd provide some warmth for my frozen digits.

The loft was small when the small bathroom, kitchen, and two closets were factored out of the square footage. There wasn't a lot of furniture or knick-knacks to go through. An empty bookshelf sat beside the twin size bed in the far corner. A floor lamp and small, very worn table huddled near the threadbare couch where Maddie must have slept on the opposite wall. A ruffled up blanket was draped onto the couch, half of it on the floor. A glass of water sat on the table with a plate bare of any crumbs.

There wasn't any place a backpack could be hiding. Still, Jake and I looked below the bed and couch, beneath the cushions and mattresses. We opened the two kitchen cabinets and peeked inside the fridge and oven. Jake even checked the pillowcases to make sure the backpack wasn't inside.

"Jake, I don't think it's here," I said, peeking behind

the curtains that looked down onto Main Street.

Jake exited the bathroom and put his gloved hands on his hips, assessing the room. "Then we work backwards in the timeline," he said.

My eyes drifted across the crumbling paint near the ceiling in thought. "Wendy?" I asked.

Jake sighed and nodded. Looking at his wristwatch he said, "Ten o'clock isn't too late for a house call, right?"

He motioned his head towards the door when I was at a loss for an answer and we went back out into the frozen town to chase down our lead.

Jake's Subaru pulled up to Wendy's house nearly thirty minutes later. The plows had not yet reached some of the streets farther from downtown and Jake's car kept swerving on the slick roads, forcing him to drive at a snail's pace. If Wendy had lived in Terryville or Sheridan, we might not have made it there until morning. Luckily, she lived on Gnarled Oaks Drive and their swanky Home Owner's Association paid to keep the streets in their subdivision clear and salted.

With determination, Jake exited the car without telling me to stay put or share his plan. Given a choice, I followed him up the perfectly snow-plowed driveway and past the candy-cane decorated pathway that lead to their front door. Large ornate wreaths covered the top half of the wooden double doors, forcing Jake to knock on the oak at an awkward angle.

A man about the same height as Jake answered the door with a heavy five o'clock shadow. "Deputy," he greeted, adjusting his glasses. "What are you doing here?"

"I'm sorry to bother you," he apologized, taking a step closer to the door. "There's been a new development in the case and I really must insist on asking Wendy a few more questions."

The man adjusted the belt on his robe as the cold air must have been attacking him in waves. "We just left this ordeal behind at the police station. My wife just got Wendy to go to sleep; she needs her rest. She really is quite shook up."

"I understand Mr. Nottingham," Jake said diplomatically. "I wouldn't ask if it wasn't important. I'd much rather impose this on you tonight, rather than waiting until tomorrow and possibly tainting your Christmas Eve."

The man frowned and opened the door wide. "Very well," he said, showing us inside. "We'll do anything to help prove Wendy's innocence."

Mr. Nottingham led us to a room that contained two couches facing each other. An ornately carved coffee table sat between them and I noticed it at once: t was one of Sadie's mom's pieces. She was a gifted woodworker and her talent glowed beneath the lights in the room. A simple glass bowl of pinecones, dried orange slices, and cinnamon sticks was the only decoration it could ask for.

"What's going on?" a petite woman, who I assumed was Wendy's mother, asked when she joined Mr. Nottingham's side.

"Wake up Wendy," he instructed, nodding toward the staircase.

"But Robert!" she protested, glancing in our direction.

"Trust me," he said, placing a hand on her arm briefly. "It will help Wendy."

She pursed her lips and turned from the room a little too brashly. "Excuse my wife," Mr. Nottingham said as he sat across from Jake and me on the couches.

ake shook his head as if he noticed nothing out of the ordinary. "This is my associate," Jake said, motioning in my direction with his hand. "Charlotte Parker." It surprised me that Jake used my proper name rather than the name everyone in town knew me by, but I let the question go as quickly as it came.

With a firm handshake he greeted me and then turned his attention back to Jake. "You must understand, Deputy, that Wendy is a good kid. She wouldn't do anything like this," he assured us.

"Yes, well, that's what we're here to do: find the facts that lead to the truth," Jake said, leaning over; his elbows balancing on his knees.

"I know you're tired, sweetie," Mrs. Nottingham said a little too loudly as she led Wendy down the stairs. "But you only have to answer a few questions and then they'll be gone and you can go back to sleep."

Wendy and her mother rounded the corner shortly after. Wendy wore a light blue robe over a pair of matching pajamas. She didn't close the robe and the sash nearly reached her fluffy slippers as she reached her father.

Sitting between her parents, Wendy rubbed her red and swollen eyes. She'd done a fair amount of crying that evening and it showed. "How come you're here?" she asked, her eyes flying between Jake and me. "I promise I haven't done anything." She turned her face to me and added, "You said you believed me!"

My heart ached at the pain in her voice. She'd been fighting all night for someone else to say they believed her. "I do, Wendy," I said, not sure if I was overstepping Jake's authority and gave him a quick glance. His face was unreadable.

"Jake—Deputy Vega," I said, quickly correcting myself. "He has some questions for you. There are a few things we need to be absolutely sure of."

Wendy bit her bottom lip and seemed to try and detect

lies in my words. Finally, she turned her attention to Jake as her mother put a protective arm around her daughter. "What is it?" she asked.

"Wendy," he began, scooting closer. "We need to know for sure: did Maddie have her backpack with her when you met her on the bike path that night?"

Wendy narrowed her eyebrows in thought. She seemed to be pushing away the sleep that desperately wanted to take hold of her. Ultimately, she nodded. "Yes," she reported. "I'm sure of it. Definitely."

"What makes you so sure?" Jake asked, listening carefully.

"When I tried stopping her, she swung around and it hit me. Knocked the wind out of me."

"She took off the backpack and swung it at you?" Jake asked, not taking his eyes off Wendy.

Wendy shook her head. "She didn't take it off. It was heavy. I mean it was always heavy and filled with books, but when I grabbed her, to stop her from running off and trying to get her back to Town Circle, she just kinda whipped around and it hit me. Knocked her off balance too. She fell to the ground. It took her a few seconds to get up, like the world was spinning and she couldn't hang on."

Jake nodded, following every word. "And you're sure it was *her* backpack?" he asked.

"Yeah," Wendy said, nodding. "Red Jansport backpack. Same one she's worn every day since I've known her. There's a keychain of a frog on the zipper."

"And you're sure she had her backpack when she left you?"

Wendy bit her lip again and thought about it. "Yeah," she said. "I was holding her from behind, but her backpack was so bulky that I couldn't reach all the way around. We fell backwards—she and her backpack right on top of me. We fell onto the ice-hard snow on the side of the trail. I hurt my back and laid there for a few moments until the pain stopped. When I looked up, I saw her disappear in the darkness ahead. That's when I chased after her but couldn't find her."

Jake licked his lips in thought. "Do you have the backpack or know where it is right now?" he asked almost hesitantly.

Wendy shook her head exaggeratedly. "I don't have it!" she said defensively. "I'd think Maddie had it when she... *you know.*"

Jake took a deep breath, digesting the information as Wendy's mother rubbed her daughter's back and her father put a protective hand on her shoulder. "Thank you, Wendy," Jake said. "You've been very helpful, and I'm very sorry we had to wake you up."

Wendy opened her mouth to say something but stopped herself. Then she blurted, "Do you believe me then?" she asked, desperately.

Jake hesitated. "I believe," he began, choosing his words carefully, "that justice comes with the truth." Wendy's shoulders slumped slightly and a frown began building in the corner of my lips. "And," he continued, slowly, "your words will help bring justice to Maddie."

My lips quickly pulled into a small but proud smile at his response. Wendy's exhaustion seemed to prevent her from grasping his message, but her parents seemed soothed by them.

"Thank you again for your time and cooperation," he said again and shook Mr. Nottingham's hand. "We'll show ourselves out."

As soon as we reached the well-lit front steps of their home, Jake turned to me with a sly smile. "I have an idea," he said and bounded down the sidewalk to his car.

Chapter Thirty-Three

SORRY TO BOTHER. I TEXTED MR. ROBINSON as Jake dropped me off at Oakie's. The store was closed, but my father was kind enough to let me eat some of the leftover steak that was on the menu of the classiest night of the year. *I need my laptop bag. Left behind in the hustle of today.*

Now? He texted back immediately. *You're crazy!*

Will forgo last paycheck to get it back 2nite. Need camera and stuff for Xmas. I responded, stuffing a heaping forkful of baked potato in my mouth.

Meet at store in 20 minutes, he responded at lightning speed.

"Tell me again," my dad said as he folded napkins at the table across from me. "What are you doing out this late, in this weather?"

I watched some of the staff taking down the black tapestry that covered the walls in their night of enchantment. "I was at the Holiday Hop," I responded, stabbing the lemon-butter drenched string beans on my plate with a fork.

"In those clothes?" he asked, raising an eyebrow.

"Long story. Jake can vouch for me," I said and took

the forkful of string beans.

"Which would explain why he dropped you off."

"See?" I said, my mouth full, "it all makes sense."

My father only lifted his eyebrows, accepting the story for what it was. "Do you want to walk home with me? I'll be another hour," he asked, checking his wristwatch.

I drained a glass of milk. "Nah. I'm meeting Mr. Robinson in twenty minutes to pick up my stuff from the store."

"This late?" my dad asked, surprise coating his words.

I nodded and put the last three pieces of meat in my mouth. "I'll see you at home, Dad. Thanks for dinner; tell Oscar it was delicious!" I reported and gave my father a quick hug before slipping out the front door.

I stood under the yellow security light at the back door of the bakery long enough for it to turn off as I waited for Mr. Robinson. Bailey's pea coat was a joke; it seemed like all it did was invite the cold night air instead of repel it. I hopped in place, breathing out warm clouds of air.

Finally, I heard Mr. Robinson's pick-up truck rumbling down the alley and the security light flashed on as he pulled into the small space between the dumpster and the building next door. I smiled in greeting, though it made no difference.

He grumbled as he fished the keys out of his pocket.

"Thanks for doing this," I said as he fumbled with the lock on the back door. He only mumbled complaints as he walked into the store and turned on one of the overhead lights. The door to the kitchen was closed and I silently sent my thoughts to Mrs. Robinson who was still in the hospital.

I made my way through the hallway and turned the corner into the dark gift shop as Mr. Robinson waited near the back door. The lights twinkling in the front window made my heart heavy, knowing the store would not know the joy of Christmas this year.

Using my cell phone as a flashlight, I quickly packed up my things—though disassembling my photography kit was not an easy task, especially in the dark.

Finally, I awkwardly navigated through the store without toppling any displays and met Mr. Robinson in the back hallway. He didn't move out of the way for me to pass, so I stopped and said, "I'm sorry for your loss, Mr. Robinson. I truly am. If there's anything I can do, please let me know."

The large man stepped to the side and said, "Just get out of here. And don't come crawling back for that paycheck either. We have a deal."

I nodded obediently. "I hope they find Maddie's backpack so your family has peace," I replied, squeezing past him. "Merry Christmas," I added, walking towards the alley.

"What do you mean, Maddie's backpack?" he asked, calling after me.

I stopped and turned, confused by his statement. "The whole town's talking about it," I said, squinting in the bright security light. "Your wife said she saw the backpack in the loft when she opened the store that morning, but Wendy swears Maddie was wearing it the night she disappeared. There's answers wherever that backpack is... or so I'm told," I explained and shrugged. "Happy Holidays, Mr. Robinson," I said lightly and disappeared into the shadows of the alleyway.

Jake was sitting in his Subaru on the corner of Oak & Main. I threw my gear into the backseat and slid into the passenger seat. "All set?" he asked.

"Hook, line, and sinker," I replied with a smile.

Seconds later, Mr. Robinson's pick-up truck pulled out

of the alley and onto Main Street. "Here we go," Jake said, putting his car into gear. I reached for the seatbelt, filled with a sudden burst of adrenaline as we followed the pick-up truck through town and onto US-16.

Keeping a respectful distance—though I'm sure Mr. Robinson didn't expect anyone following him—we ended the chase in Terryville. Mr. Robinson pulled his truck into a gravel driveway that was roughly shoveled.

Jake and I watched as Mr. Robinson walked into the house without knocking. I realized it wasn't his house when we heard yelling and the crash of broken glass. "Wait here," Jake instructed as he opened the car door.

He disappeared into the shadows on the opposite side of the house. Proudly, I adhered to his wishes for a full two minutes before my nosey Alton blood kicked me out of the car.

"This is dangerous. This is dangerous," I repeated to myself as I crept over the semi-frozen heaps of snow in Sadie's darn boots.

Silently, I crept between the bare bushes that lined the side of the house and peeked into the closest window. The blinds were open just enough for me to see a small living room, full of secondhand furniture. It seemed stale and musty—as if plopping down on the couch would send up a cloud of dust.

Mr. Robinson stood by the front door, holding a red Jansport backpack, waving it around accusingly. Nate stood several feet away, brushing away blood that dripped from his lip with the back of his hand.

"I'll give you one more chance to tell me!" Mr. Robinson exclaimed. "Tell me why YOU have this backpack!"

Nate didn't respond. Instead, he paced in front of his father-in-law slowly. I watched, trying to figure out what

I'd missed spending those two minutes in the car. Then Nate moved quicker than a piglet on Sunday and grabbed his turkey hunting gun from the corner and pointed it at Mr. Robinson.

"You crazy old man!" he yelled. "*You* gave it to me!"

Mr. Robinson's face had melted from aggression to confusion and he lowered the backpack slightly.

"You said Maddie left it in the store and you didn't want her snooping around to get it in the middle of the night," Nate explained. "You came knocking at the door at five in the morning like it was a matter of life and death! I took it from you, dropped it behind the door, and you left."

The confusion that deepened the wrinkles around Mr. Robinson's beard disappeared and his cheeks grew red. "You lying son-of-a—" Mr. Robinson spewed, taking a determined and angry step forward.

Nate shot the gun out the window beside his father-in-law in warning. The booming sound made every fiber in my body quiver from my cold perch. The thundering bang was so loud that I could barely hear the pieces of glass hitting the ground in a shower of clinks and clatters. It brought me back to that stormy October night that I was sure would be my last on earth. I fought down a bout of panic. Lights from the nearest houses turned on and illuminated the lawns. The Terryville police department would be getting several phone calls in the next two minutes.

My gaze returned to the window and I saw Jake emerge from the shadows in the kitchen, behind Nate, his weapon drawn. "Nate, I need you to put down your gun," Jake instructed. His voice was muffled from behind the glass of the window. I could see how his eyes carefully assessed the situation.

"*I* need to put down the gun?" he asked, waving the weapon carelessly. He pointed at Mr. Robinson with the gun and said, "This man is crazy! I'm doing it for my own safety!"

"I won't say it again, Nate. Put down the gun," Jake directed, taking another measured step closer.

"Ruby came home and confronted you, didn't she?" Mr. Robinson said, furious. "You knew Maddie was pregnant and you exploded like you usually do!"

Nate pointed the gun carefully at Mr. Robinson. "Watch it, old man!" he threatened.

"You couldn't control yourself," he accused, getting more and more angry with each sentence. "I bet you found Maddie that night and yelled at her for being stupid enough to get pregnant when it was *all your damn fault*!"

Pure hatred covered Nate's face; it was as if his features had transformed to a completely different person and he shot the gun again, this time out the open window. Before he could utter another word or threaten his father-in-law again, Jake gave a warning shot into the floor, feet from where Nate stood.

The hope that the gesture would diffuse the situation melted when Nate pointed the gun directly at Jake's chest. The same horrific look plastered his face. Panic overtook me and I knocked loudly on the window and ducked. When no bullet shot out the window, I picked my head up and looked inside. Jake now had Nate's gun and said, "Down on your knees, Nate."

Nate, seeing that his weapon had been confiscated, began to move in on Jake. For a split-second worry soaked through me; Nate was big and tall, like a mountain next to Jake. But without hesitation—without so much as a blink of the eye—Jake shot Nate in the leg. Right in the dirty grungy socks that covered his feet!

Nate fell in shock, and Jake wrangled him into a pair of handcuffs as if he wasn't as slippery as a bar of soap. It was so quick that Nate didn't even realize what was happening until his arms were restrained behind him. Then he exploded. A string of profanities poured out of his mouth, covered in spittle. He kicked the nearby end table with his good leg and sent the lamp and full ash tray crashing to the floor in his fit of rage.

The Terryville police broke through the front door at the sound of the crash. I'd been so caught up in making sure Jake was safe, and in awe of his skills, that I hadn't seen the flashing lights of the police cars.

Mr. Robinson was in shock, standing in the corner and hugging his granddaughter's backpack. The police had put both men in custody. "He did it!" Nate yelled, fighting the two police men who tried to restrain him. "He's a crazy old man! He did it! He'll never admit it!"

Chapter Thirty-Four

THE SUN HAD RISEN ABOVE THE HORIZON by the time I awoke on Christmas morning. The house was still, quiet, and calm; even the wind that whistled through the windows was quiet. Only the smell of banana pancakes hinted that there was movement in the house from beneath my warm covers. The excitement of Christmas morning didn't hang in the air and urge me to jump out of bed.

Yesterday was a blur of catching up on sleep and endless questions from the Gossip Club about what had happened in Terryville—and any gossip I might have gleaned from the Holiday Hop. I went to church with my family (and most of the town) and might have avoided questions, but not the stares. I wasn't sure if they were talking into their neighbor's ear about what had happened in Terryville, the drama about my ex-husband from October, or one of the many other instances I've found myself wrapped up in over the past eight months.

The rest of the family had gone to Oscar's house for their Christmas Eve buffet party. As much as I would've liked to see how my mother's veganized recipe of *kumla*—a traditional Norwegian dish—faired among the crowd, I went straight home, took a hot shower to warm my bones, and fell into bed. I was exhausted and worn down by all the talking behind my back. Thoughts of leaving cookies out for Santa (which would have pleased my dad as a midnight snack), or eating hot rice pudding before bedtime (a tradition for our family) escaped me. The magic of Christmas abandoned me this season.

Nevertheless, my stomach grumbled and it forced me to leave my bedroom. Reaching the top of the stairs, I could hear my dad, Carter, and Eli in the living room. When I reached the bottom of the stairs, I could see them putting together train tracks below the Christmas tree, in between the beautifully wrapped presents.

Behind me, the clinkering of silverware forced me to turn around. Bailey was setting the dining room table. The black sweater she wore made her blonde hair and blue eyes stand out and sparkle. I sighed, thinking about how I went to sleep with wet hair that now was probably frizzy and kinked in several spots.

"You slept in, didn't you?" Bailey asked as she set plates down at the table.

"Merry Christmas, Bailey," I said and cleared my throat. It was nearly nine in the morning, but with a young son, I guessed nine o'clock on Christmas morning was late.

"Merry Christmas, Charli," my mother chimed, her voice traveling from the kitchen. Sizzling from the frying pan followed her words. "I'm glad you're awake. Alex and Sadie should be here shortly. Will you run upstairs and change? I don't want these pancakes to get cold!"

I nodded obediently and went right back upstairs. Christmas in this house began to seem so foreign at that moment. It had been two years since I'd last celebrated with my family and then Eli was a three-year-old who could only just string together sentences and we had a small Christmas tree on the table in the dining room.

And Jackson was here.

It seemed unjustified to feel so much pain after Jackson's passing, after all the grief he'd put me through, even after his death. But I did love him. I'd wanted to build a life with him—that was why I married him. He'd become my family. All of that was gone. The image I thought my life to be—Jackson and me growing old together, celebrating our five year anniversary in Vancouver like we'd talked about on our first anniversary—it was torn away from me.

I didn't have time to get used to the idea of a life without him that divorce papers would have brought. He wouldn't still be out there somewhere after I signed those papers. He was gone forever. I would never get the chance to tell him everything I felt—the good things and the bad. So until the day I die, I'd have to lock it all away and hope that that was good enough.

As soon as I threw on a pair of black jeans and a white turtle neck that I was sure were hand-me-downs from Bailey, her voice called up the stairs, "Charli! Door!"

Experiencing a weird sense of *de ja vu*, I hopped down the stairs and heard the toy train whistling as it rumbled on its tracks. "Who is it?" I asked Bailey as she set silverware on the table.

"Jake. He's on the porch. He didn't want to come inside," she said without looking up and adjusted the pinecone centerpiece.

I slipped into my boots without fastening them, and grabbed my parka from the hall closet. Jake was dressed in his uniform as his breath billowed out in clouds from the temperature. Chills rushed down my spine as the sun hovered above the horizon and I quickly zipped my coat.

"Merry Christmas, Jake," I said and walked to where he stood by the top of the stairs. "Merry Christmas, Charli," he said. "Do you want to take a quick walk?"

I knew we were about to eat breakfast, but I didn't see Alex or Sadie's car driving up the road so I nodded. "A short one wouldn't hurt."

"Are you guys heading to church today?" he asked as we descended the stairs.

"Oh, I don't know," I admitted as we awkwardly trudged through the snow. "I have no idea what's going on lately. I'm just going with the flow."

There was no chilled breeze, which made being outside less painful. Everything seemed still and serene. It was as if the world was taking it all in before sighing at its beauty.

Jake stopped below the massive oak tree in the front yard. The tire swing was frozen, covered in the snow that had fallen in the middle of the night. "I won't be long, Charli. I have to get to the station anyway," he said, glancing in the direction of town.

"I wanted to say sorry about the other night. I cut the night short without even thinking about what it would mean to you—"

"Jake, please," I said, nearly laughing. "That's not my world. I went to The Holiday Hop to get pictures for *The Oak Leaf Press* and I got them. What we ended up doing was way more fun," I admitted and then winced when I realized my idea of fun involved guns, potential murderers, and getting in the way of danger more than once.

Jake snorted as if what I'd said was ridiculous... or comical. "I wanted to let you know that the case is closed."

"Oh?" I asked. The Alton in me had follow up questions on the tip of my tongue and I tried to restrain myself.

"Yeah. Wasn't so easy, but it's over."

"That itch gone?" I asked.

Jake chuckled. "Yeah. A witness called in with an anonymous tip that Mr. Robinson was seen at the Dead End at midnight. We followed up with the bar tender that closed the bar that night who said he was there until the bar closed at three in the morning."

"Past Maddie's estimated time of death," I pointed out.

Jake nodded. "He was well past drunk when he left the bar and somehow drove home without killing anyone."

"What about Nate?" I asked; the question almost a reflex.

"Nate was diagnosed with Intermittent Explosive Disorder in high school. He'd been taking medication since. We followed up with his doctor who said he hadn't seen or prescribed medication since 2011.

"We got him back on his meds—he *tore up* the conference room. We had to keep him in a cell until the meds kicked in. He finally confessed when he was docile enough for interrogation last night. It was one heck of a Christmas Eve."

"Confessed?" I asked. I condensed the string of questions I wanted to ask into one word.

Jake nodded. "Ruby originally told us she was sleeping that night when Maddie disappeared and said that Nate was asleep in the living room when she went to bed. That wasn't one-hundred percent true. She said that Nate had gotten extremely upset when he found out Maddie wouldn't be home that night. Ruby had locked herself in the bedroom to avoid his temper. When she woke up the next morning, he was asleep in the recliner. She said it was a normal pattern and assumed he was there all night, but for about eight hours, he had no alibi.

"Nate admitted to his lash out. He said he hated not

having Maddie under his roof—that he needed to know where she was at all times—like a 'good father,'" Jake used his fingers as quotation marks. "Around eleven o'clock he found himself in Alton Oaks. He said he'd parked the car on the street when he saw Maddie exit the alley and walk along Maple Lane. He thought she was going to meet Jason and confronted her.

"There was a struggle and Maddie kicked him pretty hard." Jake paused and seemed to carefully choose his next words, "in an area that left him incapacitated for several minutes."

"Ah," I said, understanding. It made sense now that when Wendy found Maddie, she was muttering about having to get away and kicked her in the crotch.

"When he was able to walk again, he searched for her down Main Street and looped back around on Sheridan Street. He said he came across her on the bike path." Jake's face turned dark then. His eyes narrowed as he looked towards the bare-limbed trees to the south. "He said he grabbed her and wanted to 'put her in her place.'" Again, Jake used his fingers as air quotes. His tone changed as he tried not to show too much emotion, but he was masking anger. "He pulled her behind the trees—just beside the baseball field. Maddie fought—Nate said she'd never fought that hard before. He admitted to throwing her down on the ground, but despite the amount of muscle relaxers that were in her system, she got back up and ran through the trees. He chased her. He saw her slip on the ice and fall over the edge and into the river. She broke clear through the ice." Jake paused. A hawk flew overhead; its screech broke through my stunned silence.

"He said that it was *her* fault. That if she hadn't fought him, she'd still be alive," Jake said through nearly clenched teeth. "Even on medication, after her death, he ended his confession with two words. Do you know what those two words were?" Jake asked.

I shook my head. Seeing Jake exhibit so much emotion was something I wasn't used to. Usually he wore a stoic mask while in his uniform: Work-Jake. Even Friend-Jake wasn't this emotional.

"*Stupid girl*," he said, shaking his head.

A hawk screeched above us again as I imagined Nate sitting in that conference room, his hands cuffed in front of him, his elbows resting on the table. I could just see the stubble on his chin as he shook his head, saying those two words and truly believing them.

The image of Jake sitting across from Wendy the other night in her home crossed my memory. I believed he wanted to tell her, "Yes! I believe you!" but his duty to the truth wouldn't let him. "Truth brings justice," I said, quoting him. "Nate's truth, though unsavory and downright horrible, is bringing justice."

Jake nodded in response, the anger in his features slowly melting.

"How's Mrs. Robinson?" I asked. Though what she'd done to her granddaughter was almost monstrous, she did it out of love and there was something about her that made me wish for her good health.

"She's fine," Jake said, shifting his feet. Snow crackled beneath his boots. I could feel the chill creeping into my toes as we stood in the frozen yard. "Ruby was released and went straight to the hospital."

"And Mr. Robinson?" I asked, hesitantly, as he wasn't my favorite human being.

"I guess what Nate said to him—putting the idea in his head that he killed his own granddaughter and didn't know if he really did because he was so drunk that night—it really got to him. I heard that he asked about rehab for his alcohol problem, but I don't know if he acted on it."

I made a mental note to ask Alex and Sadie if they heard anything about Mr. Robinson at the hospital when they arrived. "Are you allowed to be telling me all of this?" I asked, lifting an eyebrow.

"Probably not," he admitted more easily than I thought he would. "But if there's anyone in this world I can confide in, it's you."

I smiled at his bold and somewhat vulnerable answer. "How long are you at the station today?" I asked and noticed my brother's Jeep coming up the road.

"Nine," he said and checked his watch as my brother pulled into the makeshift driveway his and Sadie's vehicle made in the snow each time they came to visit. "Then Charlevoix gets the overnight shift. I should get going," he said as I heard the car door slam.

"Merry Christmas, Charli!" Sadie's voice sang over the snow as Alex carried a large bag of presents up the stairs.

Jake and I began climbing back over the footprints we'd made in the snow and I said, "I'll bring over some Christmas dinner later."

"That sounds amazing," he admitted.

"Are you sure you can't stay for breakfast?" I asked. "Mom made banana and chocolate chip pancakes." I could smell the maple sausage links in the air as we ended up in the flattened snow behind the Jeep.

"No, I have to make it to the station and relieve Aldridge. He has a family to get home to this morning," he said. "Merry Christmas, Charli," he said and surprised me with a hug.

All the anxiety I'd been feeling about a foreign Christmas without Jackson melted away at that moment. It really did feel like Jake and I were friends again and it was the best present I could've received. "Merry Christmas, Jake," I said and pulled away.

We turned to walk our separate directions when Jake suddenly said, "Oh! I almost forgot!"

I turned and saw him pull out an oddly-shaped present awkwardly wrapped in reindeer paper from his jacket. "Your present," he said with a smile.

I had gotten Jake something small and insignificant—a new armband for his iPod when he went running—but it was upstairs and I wasn't in a rush to give it to him. "Jake, you didn't have to," I said.

"Oh, it's nothing," he said with a sly smile.

I ripped the paper away to a metal number six—the kind you'd find at the hardware store to put up on the house as the address. I bit my bottom lip, confused. "Thanks, Jake..." I said.

He laughed at my reaction. "Because you always have my six," he said, referring to the time I was stabbed in the back and I was so high on painkillers that I told him I'd always have his back, or—as the actors in military movies would say—his six. "Don't think I didn't know it was you who knocked on the window that night," he added.

I laughed. "I love it, Jake," I said, still smiling. I felt my cheeks flush with amusement.

"Merry Christmas, Charli," he said, still in good humor.

"Merry Christmas, Jake," I replied.

I turned to face the Alton House, grasping the cold metal in my bare hand, feeling more confident to take on my first Christmas as an adult in Alton Oaks—widowed and lost, but not completely broken and alone.

About the Author

Megan Rivers is a former world adventurer and life-long writer who graduated from Northern Michigan University with a degree in writing and literature. She recently returned to live in her hometown of Evergreen Park, Illinois, with her spoiled pup Gracie. She teaches outdoor and environmental education. When not writing, she loves to visit thrift stores, bask in the outdoors, get lost in a good book, or cook delectable vegan dishes.